"You're the expert in psychology."

Jay studied her a moment before he continued, "What do you advise if someone is heading toward a situation similar to one in which he's already been badly hurt? Ignore it and wait for it to go away?"

"Not necessarily!" Dulcie assumed he was still talking about his daughter. "No two situations are exactly the same, any more than two people are exactly alike. It could end differently this time."

"So you'd advise an optimistic caution?" There was an expression on his face that puzzled her. What exactly was he driving at? Dulcie's heart started to pound.

"You could say that," she answered with a quick intake of breath.

"In that case..." Jay said softly as he pulled her close to him with a determined gentleness....

SHEILA STRUTT
is also the author of this

Harlequin Romance

2333—THE MASTER OF CRAIGHILL

On the Edge of Love

by

SHEILA STRUTT

Harlequin Books

TORONTO • LONDON • LOS ANGELES • AMSTERDAM
SYDNEY • HAMBURG • PARIS • STOCKHOLM • ATHENS • TOKYO

Original hardcover edition published in 1981
by Mills & Boon Limited

ISBN 0-373-02447-9

Harlequin edition published December 1981

CHAPTER ONE

'Jimmy, come back!' That was her voice.

'I ain't never comin' back! I hates yer! I hates the lot of yer!' That was Jimmy, screaming over his shoulder with the total anger of a ten-year-old who feels he has been betrayed as he rushed away from her down the vinyl-tiled corridor.

'Let him go! Give him time to think!' That was Gerry, stopping her at the entrance to reception as Jimmy bolted through the startled people waiting there and ran out through the plate glass front doors to became a pathetic figure rapidly disappearing along the grimy street.

Although it had all happened more than a week before, the memory of the voices built up into an unbearable crescendo in Dulcie Mortimer's head, mixing with snatches of other, later, conversations with policemen, social workers and her own boss, Gerry Herrendeen, again, all telling her that what had happened afterwards was not her fault. She could not hold herself to blame for the accidental death of a disturbed ten-year-old runaway, trying to sleep in a half demolished house when the roof caved in.

It was all too much: the memories, the nagging conviction that if only she had handled the situation differently, Jimmy Bruce might still be alive.

In an effort to outpace the sudden surge of agonising guilt that swept over her on her way home
at the end of a long working day, Dulcie at first
began to walk more quickly and then, when that
was not enough, she began to run, hearing neither the rapid tapping of her heels nor the steady
thudding of the heavy building equipment, working overtime on either side of her to demolish the
old slum houses and erect new high-rise apart-
ments in their place. All she was conscious of was
a feeling of overwhelming guilt and complete in-
adequacy.

Perhaps she really should change her job. Perhaps two years working in a child guidance clinic
in one of the poorest and most depressed areas of
north London really was long enough. Perhaps,
perhaps. . . .

The screech of brakes cut through her thoughts
like a bandsaw and she came back to the reality of
the early evening dusk to find herself standing in
the middle of a busy rush hour intersection that
she had not realised she had reached with the
front bumper of a gunmetal grey Mercedes just
brushing the hem of her tweed skirt.

She could see the driver's face, a white blur
behind the windscreen, but then the face had disappeared and a hand had gripped her shoulder
and an angry masculine voice was sounding
inches above her ear.

'Don't you ever stop to look where you're
going?'

Dulcie looked up. She hadn't seen him get out

of the car and walk towards her, but she supposed this obviously angry and tall blond man must be the driver. She also supposed that her feeling of floating two feet in the air must be the aftermath of shock and that it really was her standing there at the centre of a crowd of curious bystanders while a line of traffic was beginning to pile up behind the Mercedes in the middle of the road.

'Are you okay? I didn't hit you, did I?' The voice was gentler now; still abrupt but with its initial anger gone. It was an American voice—no, Canadian. Two years of working for Gerry, a Canadian-born psychiatrist, had taught her the subtle difference.

'No, I'm fine!' She tried to control a sudden, unaccountable fit of trembling and return the searching look of grey eyes that were concerned but, at the same time, impatient, as if her sudden unexpected appearance in front of his car had been an unwelcome interruption in their owner's ordered scheme of things. As indeed it must have been. 'I'm sorry!' she added lamely.

'You don't look fine! You're as white as a dish of watered milk! And as for being sorry, it's a little late for that!' Brushing her apology aside, her reluctant cavalier stood studying her, a good head taller and apparently completely unaware or unconcerned about the noisy line of traffic piled up behind the car.

Dulcie felt the first stirrings of recognition as he studied her. Somewhere, she was sure, she had seen him before.

'Where are you going?' he asked.

'Oh, over there!' Jolted out of her mental efforts to place him, Dulcie pointed towards the underground station on the other side of the street.

'And where from there?' he asked.

'Piccadilly Circus.'

'Right—get in! I'll drop you there—it's on my way.' He strode off towards the passenger door of the car, apparently taking it for granted that she would follow.

'No, it's all right, I can go by tube.' Piqued as much by his automatic assumption that she would accept his offer rather than by any real misgivings about his motives, Dulcie began to walk away on legs that felt decidedly rubbery. 'Thank you, anyway,' she called. 'Goodnight!'

'Don't be ridiculous!' He was back again, just as unexpectedly as before, only this time his hand was on her arm and not her shoulder and she had a strong suspicion that he would have liked to shake her.

The clinic—that was where she had seen him! He had looked just as irritated as he did now when she had burst unannounced into Gerry's office earlier that afternoon and found this sun-tanned stranger facing Gerry across the desk. Disconcerted, she had backed out before they could be introduced, but she was certain it was the same man.

'You're in no fit state to make it to the sidewalk,' he said curtly, 'far less go anywhere by tube!' The pressure on her arm increased to become the centre of a slowly spreading stream of consciousness.

'I'm perfectly all right!' Dulcie looked up and gave what she hoped was a suitably frigid glance.

'And I say you're not!' he flatly contradicted. 'Anyway, this is hardly the time or the place to discuss your physical condition.' He nodded towards the line of traffic, some of which was now beginning to squeeze past on the inside of his car. 'Come on, get in!' he ordered.

Dulcie was small—just over five feet—a fact that often caused her some frustration, particularly when young men, meeting her for the first time, misguidedly assumed they could treat her like a doll—but with this man's hand holding her arm and leading her towards the car, she not only felt tiny, she felt helpless and completely bereft of will.

He did not let her go until she was sitting in the body-contoured curves of the passenger seat, she was briefly aware of the expensive smell of leather overlaid with the faint tang of a subtle aftershave before the driver's door clicked shut and he was beside her. Acutely conscious of his presence just inches away from her, Dulcie kept her eyes fixed on the long-fingered hand resting on the gear lever as he edged the Mercedes out into the stream of traffic, changing expertly up as they gained speed and melted in with the rush hour flow.

There was a ring on his wedding finger. She shot him a covert glance. How old was he ... thirty-five? ... forty? About Gerry's age. It was hardly surprising that he was married. Obviously wealthy and undoubtedly attractive, it would have been surprising if he wasn't.

They drove down Euston Road, past the disgorging office blocks and the loaded double-decker buses, and she risked her first direct glance at his face.

It was definitely the man she had seen in Gerry's office, only then she hadn't noticed the almost feminine sweep of his eyelashes or the profile that could have been minted for an old Imperial coin. Nor, when he had turned to face her in the office, had she been able to see the way his hair swept back in a lion-like mane to brush the collar of his expensively tailored suit.

It gave him an almost predatory air, quite out of keeping with the smooth, dark worsted, and she glanced back at the hand resting on the gear lever. What was his wife like? she wondered.

He knew! The moment she looked up, he caught her eye and she realised that he had been quite aware that she had been studying him. A glint had appeared in the grey eyes and a lazy grin turned the corners of his mouth. An amusing story to tell his unknown wife! How this stupid girl, whom he would probably never see again, had first of all tried to kill herself by rushing out in front of his car and then, when he had driven her in to town to save her from herself, had sat and stared at him all the way like some sort of mesmerised rabbit.

Dulcie could guess what he was thinking. She could also hear him laughing about her with his wife, and she cursed the genetic inheritance of red hair and a translucent skin that made it so easy for her to blush.

'Do you always charge through life at break-neck speed?' The cause of her embarrassment had switched his attention back to the road.

'What do you mean?' He was easier to deal with in profile and Dulcie felt her colour beginning to subside.

'I *mean*,' he said pointedly, 'rushing into offices as if a herd of buffalo was after you and then running out in front of the nearest car as if you've got some special immunity against being killed!' It was a comment that required no answer and, after a moment, he went on, 'What do you do at the clinic, by the way?'

'I'm a psychometrist,' Dulcie returned. 'I run psychological tests on the children who are referred to the clinic for treatment.'

'A bit more important than being a secretary, I guess!' He made it sound like a subtle insult and Dulcie felt her temper begin to rise.

'Maybe, maybe not!' she said acidly. 'I do it because it happens to be something I enjoy. I'm not particularly interested in status!' She could hear the sharp edge to her voice. What an insufferable man! Just because he was a surgeon or one of the high-powered consultants Gerry occasionally called in for a second opinion on a particularly difficult case, there was no need for him to be so disparaging. 'Testing the children we see before we start treating them is a very important part of our work,' she agreed grudgingly, 'but I do it because I've always wanted to work with children.'

'Rather than produce any of your own, I suppose!' The Canadian voice held more than a hint of bitterness. 'The emancipated woman, turning her back on marriage for a career above all else!'

'Not at all! It's perfectly possible to combine the two.' That's what Ross was always telling her, anyway, although she suspected that if she succumbed to his persuasion to turn their long-standing unofficial engagement into marriage, her career would quickly become a thing of the past.

Not that she minded, but she would like to think that she could take it up again when their children were old enough not to need her fulltime presence. Their children—hers and Ross's children—she found it difficult to envisage them.

'Marriage and a career, eh?' he glanced briefly at her. 'Having your cake and eating it and not caring if both sides suffer!'

'It needn't be like that!'

He overrode her. 'A woman still expects security when she marries, but nowadays she also expects to retain her independent rights. And if one of those rights happens to be the career opportunity she's set her heart on and if marriage happens to stand in the way of it—well, what the hell!' he shrugged expressively. 'She can always get herself another husband if she ever feels so inclined, and another child or two if she really wants!'

There was more than a hint of personal experience in his bitterness and Dulcie let the subject drop. Besides, what point was there in arguing? She was never likely to see him again; it was Ross she had to convince. She turned her head away to watch the theatre lights of Shaftesbury Avenue pass by.

With his fixed ideas, her self-appointed chauffeur was the last person with whom she could discuss her doubts about marrying Ross. Once more, what was the point? She knew they would eventually get married. Everybody had always been telling her since the day, twenty years before, when the Sutherlands had moved in next door and five-year-old Dulcie and seven-year-old Ross had disappeared and put everyone in a state of panic. When they had reappeared, they were both on Ross's bicycle with Dulcie in the saddle, waving like a queen, and Ross pedalling happily up the drive.

She couldn't remember the incident, but her mother and Ross's mother could, and it seemed as if they had been predicting a wedding ever since. It wasn't that she didn't love Ross, she told herself. She just wished they had been given the opportunity to make up their own minds.

'Is this okay for you?'

Dulcie came up out of her trance to find that

they had drawn up outside the main entrance to Piccadilly Circus Underground.

'Yes, it's fine.' She found herself scanning the passing crowds, looking for Ross's dark head. Ross would have questions to ask if he saw her arriving in a car like this and in such company, and she was strangely reluctant to answer them. But of course, having been driven into town rather than coming in on the tube, she was earlier than usual and Ross would not be there. Dulcie relaxed.

'Are you meeting someone, Miss——er——?' The man at her side claimed her full attention with the directness of his question.

'Mortimer,' she said, for some reason, beginning to blush. 'Dulcie Mortimer. And yes, I am. I'm meeting a friend.'

Why had she said that? She was appalled. Although they hadn't bought the ring, it was an understood thing that one day she and Ross would marry, so why had she said that Ross was just a friend? Surely she did not want to give this obvious male chauvinist the impression she was free. He might be attractive, but she wasn't ever likely to see him again unless it was fleetingly at the clinic—and he was also, she firmly reminded herself, already married.

'A friend, eh?' He studied her. 'I won't ask male or female, but I'm glad there's someone on the scene to stop your headlong rush to self-destruction! I'll say goodnight, then.'

The hardness of muscle under the deceptive

smoothness of his suit brushed against her as he leaned across to open the door, and she got quickly out on to the pavement and bent down to say goodbye.

'Thank you for the ride. I'm sorry if I caused you any trouble!'

'No trouble at all!' His hint of sarcasm bothered her. 'Goodnight then, Miss Dulcie Mortimer.'

'Goodbye!' She said it too decisively and her last sight of him was of him leaning across with one hand on the door, looking up with an expression of faint mockery on his face, and then the door clicked shut and a whole lifetime's income for the average working woman pulled smoothly away from the curb. No wonder he didn't approve of married women working! His wife would have no need to work if he could afford a car like that!

She looked around for Ross, wishing for the millionth time that she was taller than even high heels could make her, craning her neck to see around the passing crowds but glad that Ross was not in sight. Her encounter with Gerry's Canadian consultant friend had left her unaccountably disturbed. It would be too facile to say she didn't like him. It was both more and less than that. Someone like that could overturn the direction of her life.

She pushed her way through the crowds and found a spot to wait near the entrance to the station. What was she thinking of? He couldn't change her life—she didn't even know his name.

It wasn't until she could see Ross making his way through the crowds towards her that the thought struck her. For the first time in a week, she had gone for more than half an hour without once thinking of Jimmy Bruce.

CHAPTER TWO

EVEN when the plane took off and Ross and her parents were already indistinguishable in the crowd of spectators watching from the observation lounge at London Airport, Dulcie could still hardly believe that it was happening to her.

Far from being a high-powered medical consultant, called in to give an opinion on a case, Dulcie's self-appointed chauffeur had turned out to be Gerry's lifelong friend, and now she was on her way to Canada for three months as companion to his twelve-year-old daughter.

'And don't think it'll be a holiday,' her boss had warned her. 'Jay's divorced and embittered and Lori's devoted to her father, so she hates all women for his sake. She'll also punch you out if you call her Laurel or suggest that she wear a dress instead of pants!'

'Gerry, I can't possibly go!' Dulcie pleaded.

He lit his pipe and watched her through the smoke. 'I don't think you've got much choice, have you?'

Dulcie had no reply. When Gerry had called her into his office that morning and explained just how much her work had been suffering because of what she saw as her guilt over Jimmy

Bruce's death, she had been shocked. But when he had told her that he had hired a temporary replacement and was insisting she take at least three months' leave of absence, the void this had opened up had been appalling.

What would she do with all that empty time? She knew she could go back to her parents' home in the Surrey village just outside London. She also suspected that Ross's solution would be that they get married straight away, and somehow this had alarmed her more than anything else. One day she would marry Ross, but not now—not yet.

Gerry must have suspected more than she had guessed, because that was when he had made his suggestion about Canada. Gerry was the one person with whom she had discussed her doubts about marrying Ross. More of a friend than a boss to both of them, he was also the one person whose advice Ross would take about this break in another country, with nothing to remind her of Jimmy Bruce, as being the best thing for her.

'Well,' Gerry said finally, tamping down the tobacco in his pipe and using yet another match to get it going, 'do I call Jay and tell him that you're coming or not?'

'You're sure he wants me?'

'He suggested it.'

That had been two weeks ago and since then so much had happened that Dulcie sometimes had difficulty in remembering whether it had been two weeks, two years or two days, but now she was on the plane, and the next time the huge jet touched down she would be in Canada.

The plane finished its climb and the seat belt and no smoking signs went out. Dulcie unclipped her belt and settled back. They still had Scotland to cross and then the long haul west across the Atlantic before they flew over Canada's northern boundary and started the last leg of the journey south to Winnipeg in the middle of the prairies.

The letter she got out of her bag dropped open at the folds and she re-read it for the umpteenth time. Jason Maitland III—the man Gerry called Jay—was confirming that she would be spending three months at Rose Valley Ranch as companion to his twelve-year-old child.

Not 'daughter', Dulcie had noticed immediately the letter had arrived, but 'child', and this tied in with everything Gerry had told her.

Jason Maitland III, whose grandfather had lost everything in the Wall Street crash of 1929 but whose father had salvaged an undistinguished piece of land in the prairie country of Saskatchewan and built it up into the multi-million-dollar ranching enterprise stretching over thousands of square acres that Jay ran today.

Jay and Gerry had met in high school, but their paths diverged when Gerry married an English girl and settled in London and Jay married a young American movie actress—'the most beautiful creature you ever saw', according to Gerry—and took her to live in his prairie empire. The marriage had ended a month after Lori had been born, with Jay's wife desperate to get away from the isolation of the ranch and back to her career in Hollywood.

Dulcie remembered Jay's caustic comments about a woman expecting the right to have a career with marriage. She also remembered the bitterly cynical expression on his hard, handsome face and the first of many misgivings had filled her head.

Divorced and with a baby daughter, Jay had withdrawn even further into his private empire, living there with Lori and a few Indian hands to do the work. Jay travelled, but at Rose Valley it was a man's world. Whatever contact he had with women was kept well away both from his home and from his daughter, and this was the prospect facing her as the plane droned on over the Atlantic.

Dulcie slipped the much folded letter back into the envelope and glanced at the photograph Gerry had given her of the little girl he called his 'adopted niece.' It could have been a picture of a boy, and there was more than a hint of the father's arrogance in the face that stared back at her.

And that was why she was sitting in this plane, letting the miles slip past that would take her to Saskatchewan. Not because of the father, Dulcie hurriedly reminded herself, but to inject a little feminine example into a young girl's life before she hit the real problems of adolescence.

It was crucial that Lori have some contact with a woman, Gerry had emphasised. And by insisting that she take a three-month break from the clinic, he had also made sure that one Dulcie Mortimer had no alternative but to supply it.

Dulcie dozed and slept and watched a film she had already seen before—no better thousands of feet above ground level—and ate a plastic meal from a plastic tray. A meal with two desserts, she thought at first, but then she remembered the North American liking for fruit with a green salad and identified one portion as having cottage cheese and a little lettuce and the other as having cream. Thank goodness Air Canada didn't go in for marshmallows, she thought wryly, remembering the taste shock of biting into a savoury-looking confection one night when Gerry's wife had invited her and Ross to dinner and finding that she was eating a marshmallow salad with her roast beef.

The meal was over when the plane flew into a sudden change of atmospheric pressure and the sudden turbulence made her look out of the window. They had crossed the Atlantic and Canada was far beneath them. Miles and miles of barren, empty tundra, black and white with snow still lingering in pockets even though it was early June. She was nearing journey's end and she felt the first jolt of excitement mixed with apprehension. But it was too soon to get nervous. Canada was a vast country and although they had already flown thousands of miles there were thousands more to go before they reached the Canadian heartland and the plane started its long descent to Winnipeg International Airport. Her second meeting with the man who set all her inner alarm bells ringing was still hours away.

Even when the plane load of passengers had

dispersed, Dulcie was still standing between her two suitcases and looking around the rapidly emptying concourse. She needn't have been in Winnipeg. She could have been in any airport in the world and her only problem was that she was here, thousands of miles away from anyone she knew, and no one seemed to give a damn!

She pushed back the mass of chestnut curls that a whim of fashion had made all the rage and gazed around the airport with bleak green eyes as uneasiness began to overtake her anger. Surely Jason Maitland III had not had a change of heart and decided not to meet her?

'You Dorothea?' The flat, clipped voice came from somewhere above her head, startling her as much with its unexpectedness as by its abrupt use of her full name, and Dulcie looked up at the tallest North American Indian she had ever seen in her life. The *only* North American Indian she had ever seen in the flesh in her life!

'Yes, that's right.' She studied the classic, flat brown features, the straight, shoulder-length brown hair and the feather stuck in the leather band around the sweat-stained cowboy hat. 'Have you got a message for me from Mr Maitland?' she asked hopefully.

'Jay sent me to fetch you. These yours?' He bent his immense height and considerable width towards the cases on the floor.

'Yes, but . . . .' Dulcie hesitated. She knew he was going to find this stupid but, quite suddenly, the idea of going off into the blue with him was

frightening. 'Have you got anything to prove that
Mr Maitland sent you?' she asked warily.

'No, ma'am, I ain't!' The leather fringing on
his jacket ripped as he straightened with her luggage. 'But I can tell you one thing. I wouldn't be
here unless he had, that's for sure!'

He looked around the modern airport with an
expression of utter distaste and Dulcie felt extremely foolish.

'Oh, yes, I see,' she said lamely. 'Then I suppose we'd better go.' She turned towards the
main exit in an effort to cover her embarrassment.

'Not that way.' The Indian was using one of
her heavy cases to point casually towards a smaller side door. 'The plane's out back.'

Indians rode horses and raided wagon trains:
they did not pilot aeroplanes. That, at least, was
what Dulcie had always thought until she found
herself sitting next to Lloyd Southwind as the
four-seater Cessna took off. He had told her his
name while they had been waiting on the runway
for permission to leave. He had also told her he
was Jay's foreman and that Jay owned the twin-
engined plane, but, other than those reluctant nuggets of information, he had said nothing. On the
ground, he had restricted his conversation to
communication with the airport control tower
and, as he flew, he looked straight ahead. Glancing at his impassive profile, Dulcie got the strong
impression that Jay's foreman probably shared
his employer's opinion about women, and she

was once more swept by a great wish that she had not come.

After the huge jumbo jet, her first experience of flying in a small plane was scarey. The noise was deafening and for a long while she was convinced that any sudden movement would destroy their balance and send them tumbling from the sky, but, as the Cessna went steadily on, she began to relax and feel able to look down.

They were flying west and a little north over what seemed like solid forest until suddenly, as if someone had drawn a line, the forest stopped and there was only open prairie. It went on for miles and miles, all shades of green and brown under the hot June sun, divided into huge squares by the roads and with the occasional farm or little railhead town appearing on the horizon and gradually passing underneath them.

They flew on and on until a stretch of brilliant green appeared ahead of them, a little to one side of a house, and a cluster of outbuildings set in a semi-circle of trees and Lloyd Southwind banked and brought the plane into the breeze that tugged at the scarlet air-sock to make a perfect landing on the Rose Valley landing strip.

Her ears still ringing from the engine noise, Dulcie sat there until the door beside her was pulled open and a much younger Indian stood in the shadow of the wing, grinning up at her with a mouth full of pointed yellow teeth. His smile and the way he tipped his hat before he offered her his hand to help her down were the first welcoming things she had seen since she had arrived in Canada.

'It's this way, ma'am,' he said. 'Watch your head.'

'Thank you.' Dulcie gratefully returned his smile as he shielded her head with his hand to make sure she did not hit the wing struts. 'But what about my luggage?' she asked when Lloyd Southwind made no move to hand it out.

'He'll fetch that.' The boy nodded towards another man in cowboy hat and jeans who was walking slowly up towards the plane. 'This way, ma'am.'

Dulcie followed him. There was still no sign of Jay. He had probably decided that it was beneath his dignity to come out and meet a woman, to say nothing of the risk of giving her the misguided idea that he was pleased to have her there.

'Over here, ma'am.' The Indian boy had walked ahead of her, he sounded anxious, and, as she hurried to catch up, Dulcie had her first look at the house.

It was dazzling; a three-sided bungalow painted white and surrounded by the barns, out-buildings and stock corrals of a big cattle ranch-ing operation. But even though it was so large, Rose Valley seemed no more than a speck in the miles and miles of prairie all around it and the lawn stopped abruptly, with no fence, as if who-ever had planted it had realised the impossibility of making any real mark on such immensity and had given up.

There was a full-sized swimming pool on the lawn and a motorcycle had been abandoned on the grass beside it, but the water, dancing and shimmering in the brilliant light, made Dulcie's eyes play tricks and when they went inside, the sudden transition from light to dark left her with only the vaguest impression of a big, untidy entrance hall before her guide was hurrying her down one of the two dark corridors leading from the hall and opening another square of brilliant light. He stood aside and she walked in to what was obviously a bedroom. Her bedroom! The one place she had any right to call her own for the next three months.

The vague impression of dust and clutter in the entrance hall persisted here, except that here it was the air of sterile emptiness that struck her. The room might be large and the furniture impressive and fairly free of dust, but there was not one welcoming touch; no hint that anybody cared. It was all as impersonal and remote as a room in an out-of-the-way hotel.

If she had needed a reminder that in coming to Rose Valley she had come to a man's fiercely protected private world, this was it. And not only that, the ruler of this particular empire had so far shown every sign of wishing that she wasn't there!

'You've got your own washroom, ma'am. It's through here.' The Indian boy was starting to open a connecting door when another voice cut in from behind them.

'That's fine, Mike, I'll take care of all the rest.'

Dulcie spun round. If she had been able to see him properly she might have guessed, but her eyes were still confused by the sudden transition from light to dark and then light again, and all she could see was the silhouette of a man standing in the doorway with her suitcases on the floor at his feet.

She was suddenly very angry. The boy called Mike had been the first person to show her the slightest sign of courtesy, far less friendship, since she had set foot in Canada, and she was determined not to let him be sent away and replaced by this ... this ... boor, who was standing there as if he owned the place.

'I'd rather Mike showed me round, if that's all right!' Dulcie heard the note of English missishness in her voice and could have sworn the man was smiling if only she had been able to see him properly. Instead she turned to Mike, ignoring him. 'Where did you say the bathroom was?' she asked.

For answer, Mike just looked at her. Then he looked at the man at the door. 'He'll tell you!' All the welcoming inflection in his voice was gone and he left the room, circling around the man at the door, without a backward glance.

The man nodded and took a step towards her, halving the distance that separated them in that one stride, and Dulcie started to get alarmed.

'I warn you that if you come any closer, I'll speak to Mr Maitland!' She was saying all the wrong things, she knew she was, but there was an air of purpose about this man that frightened her.

'So you'll tell Mr Maitland, will you?' Far from stopping him, he was suddenly so close that even her dazzled eyes could not mistake his face.

Grey eyes without a hint of softness, harsh lines against a deeply tanned skin and blond hair that she had last seen grazing the collar of an expensive worsted suit now even longer and curling down on to the collar of a plaid work shirt.

She was not looking at the man but at the master. She was looking up at Jay himself!

He was younger than she remembered, a few years less than forty, probably no more than thirty-five, and his eyes, which she had studiously avoided meeting in the car, appeared to have a disconcerting ability to change from light to dark depending on his mood. She had been left with an impression of sunflecked grey when she had got out of the Mercedes in London and Jay had been smiling ironically up at her, but now he was not smiling and his eyes were dark. With his mane of hair and his lips drawn slightly back from his teeth, he reminded her suddenly of a prairie lion. One of the grey lynxes that, she had read, still roamed wild up north.

Conscious of hard chest and stomach muscles only a breath away, she started to step back, but the sudden, strong flexing of fingers on her shoulders stopped her and she was forced to stand and endure the close scrutiny of an inspection that held everything except acceptance.

'So you're really here,' he finally said quietly. 'I half expected you to cry off.'

'Why should I?' It was hard to maintain any sort of composure with his fingers digging into her shoulders and his eyes boring into hers. No one had ever treated her like this before or made it so clear that her presence was unwanted. 'I promised Gerry that I'd come and I also got your letter. Why should you think I'd change my mind?'

'Because you're a woman—a member of a sex not exactly noted for its consistency!' His lips curved in a parody of a smile, but the fractional relaxation of his fingers gave Dulcie the chance to pull away, relieved to have the extra space between them.

'As you seem to have such a poor opinion of my sex,' she said on the basis of the courage that distance gave her, 'I'm surprised you even sent Lloyd to Winnipeg to meet me. If you'd left me there, I might have gone straight back home!'

'The thought did cross my mind,' he admitted calmly. 'But by that time it was too late to change things.'

He stood there studying her until the light floral dress her mother had insisted that she wear rather than her much more practical linen trouser suit seemed to disappear and Dulcie felt herself blushing to the roots of her chestnut curls.

'I hope you're satisfied with what you see, at least!' she said with another attempt at sarcasm.

'Quite satisfied! You're exactly as I remember

you—an attractive, not to say lovely woman.' He repaid her with an infuriating smile before his face hardened and his voice took on a hurtful note. 'But then appearances aren't everything, are they? They're important to make that first good impression but, deep down, all any woman's interested in is how to turn that first good impression to her advantage. Manipulate a situation that she's deliberately and artificially created with her beauty and her charm to her own benefit!' His lips twisted cynically. 'What you were saying once about a woman's right to have a career as well as marriage is a good enough case in point. Find a man who's fool enough to fall in love and give you the security of marriage while you build up your career, and then leave him without a second thought when your career begins to prosper and marriage interferes. In other words,' he snapped, 'take everything and give as little as you can give back!'

She knew that he was talking about his marriage, but the urge to fight back was irresistible and she could not fight it down as she had done when the subject had come up between them in London.

'That's ridiculous!' she protested. 'You're making every woman out to be the same, and that's not true! Not all women are totally career-minded.'

'Aren't they?' he rapped. 'Then why are you here? Isn't the only reason because otherwise you wouldn't have a job?'

'I'm here because Gerry insisted I take a break from the clinic,' Dulcie admitted, wondering how much Gerry had told him and wishing he hadn't said so much. 'But I'm here mainly because you asked me to come,' she added, remembering the much folded and re-read letter in her bag.

He ignored his own part in getting her to Rose Valley. 'Gerry was wrong, dead wrong,' he told her bluntly. 'Friends sometimes have a lot to answer for when they interfere. Somehow he persuaded me that if Lori didn't have a woman's influence in her life now, she would have real problems when she grew up. But Lori doesn't need another example of how women behave and think!' His voice cracked harshly. 'She's already had her mother's!'

It was almost as if the sight of her standing in his house had brought all the bitterness he had repressed boiling to the surface. There was no other way Dulcie could account for an explosion of feeling that was as raw and as real as if his wife had left him yesterday and not almost twelve years earlier. She suddenly felt utterly exhausted. The effects of Jay's bewildering and incredibly hostile reception, coming on top of her long transatlantic flight, were beginning to have their effect. She had come through so many changing time zones that she no longer knew what time it was; all she knew was that it seemed as if she had never been to bed. She caught hold of the nearest chair.

'Now that you've made it clear that you bitterly

regret being forced into the situation of having to have me here,' she said wearily, 'perhaps you'd be kind enough to give me time to unpack a few things and freshen up. If you really want me to leave, I'll go in the morning, Mr Maitland!'

'Call me Jay.' If he had noticed her sudden wave of tiredness or realised what an effort it was to stand and face him, he gave no indication. 'But if you think a first name means anything, forget it,' he added quickly. 'Everyone's on first name terms out here. It didn't need you to arrive tricked out to look your most feminine and beguiling,' he glanced at her dress again and at her strappy high-heeled sandals, 'to get me to ask you to call me Jay!'

It was the last straw. If what he had been doing was to deliberately insult her so that she would turn tail and leave almost before she had set foot inside the house, then he had succeeded.

'I really don't think there's any point in going on with this—*Mr* Maitland,' she said icily. 'You've obviously not only made up your mind about the sort of person I am but also about my motives for being here. I'm sorry for your daughter, I really am, if she's got all your inbuilt prejudices against women to contend with as she grows up, but I really don't think my staying here can possibly do any good. I'll leave tonight!'

There was what seemed an infinitely long silence as he stood and studied her. Was he going to back down or was he going to jump at her ultimatum? There was no way of telling from the brooding, almost regretful, expression on his face, and although she still meant every word she'd said, Dulcie suddenly wished she had not been quite so quick to admit defeat.

'I told you to call me Jay,' he said eventually. 'And how are you going to get back to Winnipeg?' He paused in the open doorway on his way out. 'Walk?'

It took five minutes of measured breathing and walking aimlessly around the room willing herself not to scream before Dulcie could be sure that she had recovered her self-control. Arrogant, self-centred, embittered and prejudiced—all of these went some way to describing Jay Maitland III, and yet none of them totally summed him up. There must be another side to the hostile, aggressive personality he chose to present to the world—at least to that part of it that happened to be female—but she doubted if she would ever uncover it. And, for the time being at least, he had her trapped.

His pointed comment about the distance to Winnipeg had reminded her just how isolated the ranch was and how dependent she had made herself by coming there, but she was still determined to find a way out of this the impossible situation that she had let Gerry talk her into just as soon as she possibly could.

There was a gentle knocking on the door and Dulcie jumped, even though she knew it would not be Jay. He would most certainly not knock gently; he probably wouldn't knock at all.

'Ma'am!' The door opened slightly and Mike's head appeared round the edge. 'Jay told me to ask you if you wanted supper in your room or if you'll be eating with him?'

'Will Laurel be eating with her father?' Dulcie was quite sure that Jay hadn't put the message so politely. 'Go and ask that damn woman where she wants to eat!' would have been more like him.

'Lori?' Mike's face lit up. 'Sure, she'll be there.'

'Then tell Mr Maitland I'll eat with them.' She might as well make the most of the opportunity to meet the child who had been responsible for bringing her to Rose Valley, even though she was unlikely to be there long enough to make any impression on Lori's life. 'What time is supper?' Dulcie asked.

'Oh, 'bout thirty minutes.' Mike gave a facial shrug as though time was not of much account and disappeared.

Thirty minutes! Dulcie looked at her watch. Two in the morning by that but about seven in the evening here. Lord, but she was tired! She had been awake and travelling for almost twenty-four hours.

She had done some unpacking and had showered in the bathroom leading from her room which was, surprisingly, equipped with everything she could need from a pile of expensive fluffy towels down to a complete range of bath salts, oils and scented, handmade soap, when the noise of an engine travelling fast took her to the window.

Her bedroom was at the back and in the centre of the bungalow, overlooking the windbreak of tall trees with a strip of well watered and mown grass in between and, as she stood there, a motor-bike came tearing into her field of vision, ripping tracks across the grass as the rider put out a leg to keep the machine on balance and then raced past her window to disappear around the far corner of the house with a screech of tires and a puff of blue exhaust smoke.

The incident surprised her. Although Jay had told her that everyone was on first name terms, it still surprised her that he allowed equality to go so far that his employees felt free to race their bikes across the lawns, especially as someone—presumably on Jay's instructions—obviously worked so hard to keep them in such immaculate condition. She looked with regret at the furrows the bike had torn across the velvety surface and turned away. Jay's relationship with his employees was entirely his concern. She had quite enough to worry about over her relationship with the man himself, to say nothing of his daughter.

'This is my daughter.' Jay was waiting for her when she went into the hall which seemed to act as the main living room of the house, and he had his hand on the shoulder of a tense young figure dressed entirely in black.

Dulcie had the impression that if the hand had not been there, the girl would have bolted, and she had to remind herself that she *was* looking at a girl, because what she was seeing was the boy who had raced past her window on the motorbike.

'Hello, Laurel.' Dulcie heard her own long skirt rustling on the parquet floor as she went towards them.

'My name's Lori.'

The face almost on a level with her own regarded her inimically, with her father's eyes set under dark, straight brows.

Dulcie mentally kicked herself and held out her hand. 'Lori, then,' she said, smiling. 'How do you do?'

Lori stared back at her.

Don't rush it, Dulcie warned herself silently. Acceptance is a fragile, hardwon thing, and she had three months to gain acceptance from this hostile, boyish figure with its dark curly hair.

Three months! What was she thinking of? She didn't have three months. She didn't have any time at all if things continued as they had begun.

'Hi!' Dulcie thought she saw the fingers on Lori's shoulder tighten before Lori answered in a small, resentful voice, but her proffered hand was totally ignored and Lori turned her face away, a miniature of her father in stance, attitude and hostility. The only difference was that whereas Jay's hair was blond, the hair curling down on to the collar of Lori's black leather jacket was almost as dark as the jacket itself. They both had the same grey eyes, though; Jay's studying her as if curious to see how she would deal with this new situation and Lori's studiously turned away.

'I've heard a lot about you from Mr Herrendeen.' Dulcie had a sudden unaccountable urge to acquit herself well and she was the one who broke the extended silence. 'What do you call him, Uncle Gerry?'

'No, Gerry,' Lori said.

'I told you we were all on first name terms out here.' There was a glint in the older pair of grey eyes watching her and the suspicion of a smile. Jay was enjoying her discomfort and his evident amusement made Dulcie say the last thing she should have said.

'I think I saw you riding your bike just now, Lori.' She had been seeking some reaction and she got it, but it was definitely not the reaction she had planned.

'I told you, she's a fink! I saw her standing at her window spying on me!' Lori Maitland's face was filled with as much animation as anyone could have wanted. The only problem was that it was sheer blazing anger and contempt and she was looking up at her father, not at Dulcie, and willing him to take her side. 'I told you not to let her come here, Dad!' she said passionately. 'We've got each other! We don't need her!'

'That's enough!' Jay's voice was icy. 'You'll apologise to Dulcie and then you'll take yourself off to your room. And first thing tomorrow, you'll be out back seeing what you can do to repair the damage you did to the lawn. I don't have Mike spend hours on it just to have you rip it up when the fancy takes you! Now, apologise!'

It was wrong, all wrong. For an instant Dulcie had thought that Jay might be making amends for his own rudeness earlier when he had stopped his daughter, but by going on and imposing punishment, he had done the worst thing he could have done. Lori would go to her room convinced that Dulcie was the cause, and that would make the gap between them even more difficult to bridge.

'Apologise!' While Dulcie was struggling to find the right thing to say to save the situation, Jay was insisting.

'I'm sorry!' The voice was low and sulky and there was a moment when Dulcie thought that Jay was going to insist on more, but the fingers on the shoulder of the leather jacket slackened and Lori wrenched herself away. Dulcie knew what she was feeling; she, too, had felt the numbing pressure of those fingers on her arm.

'Now go to your room!' Jay was dealing even more harshly with his daughter than he had with her and Dulcie wondered if she was the only one to see the look of pleading that Lori sent in his direction before, without another word, she swung round on a leather-booted heel and went off down one of the two passages leading from the hall. It didn't take much imagination to realise that the defiantly squared shoulders would crumple immediately they were out of sight and that there was a good chance that Lori Maitland would cry herself to sleep.

'I really didn't take it too personally, you know,' Dulcie spoke above the slamming of a distant door. 'There wasn't any need to send her to her room!'

Jay looked down at her and there was a second's pause. 'Don't take equality too far,' he warned. 'You may be an emancipated woman, but I say what's going to happen in my house!'

Mike's arrival with the announcement that 'food was on the table' saved Dulcie from a retort that, judging by the way Jay handled opposition, could have had her spending her first night at Rose Valley out on the prairie.

Dinner was like a scene from *Giant* or any one of the films about the life and loves of Texas oil barons and ranchers that Dulcie had seen in black and white on television, except that this was Canada and she was sitting at one end of a long, badly polished table, with Jay at the other and Lori's place conspicuously empty at one side.

As well as looking after the house and garden, Mike, it appeared, was also the cook, and the steak he put in front of her hung over on either side of her plate, reminding her too vividly of the animal it came from for her to be able to eat. Jay scarcely spoke and the only time he came alive was when Lloyd Southwind came in, tossing his hat on the floor and using his foreman's prerogative to sit casually down in Lori's place and eat the large steak and mound of french fried potatoes that Mike produced for him.

Dulcie's determination to find a way out of the impossible situation into which she had been manoeuvred grew as she half listened to a conver-

sation about beef prices and bushel yield, but her
only reaction when Lloyd finally left was relief
that this interminable day would soon be over
and she could go to bed. Her relief, however,
turned into wary apprehension when Jay got up
and walked slowly down the length of the table in
her direction.

'You must be tired.'

She had braced herself for criticism, hostility,
anything except the note of unexpected concern,
even tenderness, that burred his voice.

'I am.' She looked up at him and smiled and
for some extraordinary reason, her heart stuck in
her throat. 'I'm sorry about Lori,' she said
quietly. 'We seem to have got off on the wrong
foot.'

He studied her. Her skin paler even than the
cream silk of her blouse; her eyes huge and shadowed with weariness and her hair, with the soft
light of a single table lamp behind her, aureoled
in a haze of misty red curls.

'Don't worry.' She scarcely felt him move her
heavy chair or knew that she stood up. All she
knew was that she was standing close to him and
that a part of him was reaching out to a deep
inner part of her. 'It's a new situation for all of
us,' Jay went on softly. 'We've all got a lot to
learn.'

CHAPTER THREE

JEANS. That was what she would wear that morning. With a tailored white shirt and maybe even a scarf to fill in the neckline. Anything not to encourage Jay to touch her again.

She wouldn't think about the reason why she was taking this precaution, any more than she would think about the tremor that had run through her when Jay had softly traced the outline of her face with an almost disbelieving finger before turning abruptly away with a brief goodnight.

It had been a simple, totally sexless gesture and yet it had aroused her more than anything Ross had ever done. Ross, the man she was going to marry, and who was planning to make a trip to his company's head office in Calgary so that he could spend some time with her during the three months she expected to be away.

Ross was a chemical engineer, working for a big international oil consortium, and Calgary was only a few hundred miles from Rose Valley. A mere step in Canadian terms, Ross had assured her, the night before she left.

Dulcie finished knotting the scarf around her neck. It was ridiculous to place so much import-

ance on what had happened the previous night,
especially as she suspected that Jay's purpose had
been to test her, to prove that all women, like his
wife, were susceptible to a man's admiration.
Why else had he let her go when she began to
tremble and why else had his face hardened in the
instant before he had turned away?

She had no reason to suppose he found her
presence at Rose Valley any more acceptable now
than he had when she arrived, and some time that
day she was going to have to decide if she was
going to insist that he make arrangements to have
her flown back to Winnipeg so that she could
catch the next transatlantic flight home. But she
would do that later. For now, she would go and
get her breakfast.

The dining room which had looked so gloomy
and overpowering the night before was even more
depressing in the daylight than it had been when
the lamps were lit. Dust hung over everything,
dancing in the sunshine streaming in through the
faded colourless curtains and settling in a fine
layer on the furniture. And the furniture, although obviously valuable and mostly antique,
was marked and scratched and badly in need of
care and polish. The general air of neglect and
lack of interest could not have been more in keeping with the all-male household Jay had ordered
for himself, and Dulcie wondered if a woman had
ever been allowed to set foot in it since the day
his wife had left.

As well as being gloomy and depressing, the

room was empty, with no sign of Jay or Lori—surely Jay's idea of punishment didn't extend to Lori missing breakfast as well?—but there was a glass of orange juice at the place on the long table where Dulcie had sat the night before and she sat down again.

She had noticed when she had been dressing that someone had started to repair the tire tracks on the lawn outside her window, so Lori must be about.

' 'Morning, ma'am!' Dulcie reacted to the footsteps a moment before she heard the voice and her breathing was hurried and uneven when Mike came in carrying a plate.

'Good morning.' Dulcie smiled up at him. There was dirt on the chef's apron that he was wearing over his shirt and jeans and the hands that put the loaded plate in front of her were none too clean. The thought that he had stopped off from some outside chores to cook her breakfast flashed through her mind.

Mike, however, clearly saw nothing wrong and his brown, high-cheekboned face was one big grin of satisfaction and eagerness to please as he stood back from her chair.

'I guessed you'd be hungry, 'cos you ate nuthin' last night,' he said proudly, 'so I fixed you the works. Yell if there's anything else you want. Kitchen's just next door!' He nodded in the general direction of the wall.

'I don't think there will be.' Dulcie studied her plate. 'This looks . . . er . . . great!'

'Sure thing!' Mike was satisfied and he left the room, tracking dirt from his pointed cowboy boots across what had once been a fine Oriental carpet and could be again, if only it was cleaned.

The orange juice had been delicious, freshly squeezed and icy cold, but when Dulcie looked at the breakfast Mike had produced with such great pride, her stomach began to curl around the edges.

When Mike had said 'the works', that was exactly what he had meant. There was steak; not as large as the one the night before but steak nevertheless, oozing a reddish gravy across two fried eggs and a pile of fried potato sitting in a pool of grease. Didn't these men eat anything but steak? Dulcie longed for toast and marmalade.

'Good morning!' This time they were really Jay's footsteps and Dulcie's breathing once more began to play tricks as he came in wearing close-fitting faded denims and a denim shirt that strained across the powerful muscles of his chest. He walked across to the heavily carved and dusty sideboard and began to pour thick black coffee from an automatic coffee maker that she hadn't noticed before. 'Do you want coffee, or would you prefer tea?' He looked at her directly for the first time, glancing over his shoulder with thickly lashed grey eyes and making her more aware of herself than she had ever been with any man in her life.

'Coffee, please!' The words came out unnaturally loudly and Dulcie looked down, careful not to let her eyes rise above the level of a broad, silver-buckled belt as long, competent fingers poured a second cup and carried it across. There was a clean, fresh outdoor smell mixed with the smell of coffee as the cup was set down in front of her and then footsteps were going away across the carpet and a chair scraped back and creaked underneath his weight. Dulcie let out her breath in a long, careful sigh. It was safe to look up now, but she kept her eyes fixed on her plate.

'Mike! Where's my breakfast!' Jay sounded impatient.

'Coming, boss!' Mike's voice floated through the hatch leading to the kitchen over a sudden urgent rattling of plates.

Jay began to stir his coffee. Still looking at her untouched meal, Dulcie could feel him watching her and the tension crackled along her nerves.

When he finally broke the silence, it was with a question. 'Did you sleep well?'

'Yes, I did.' Deep and dreamless for the first time in weeks, untroubled by guilt over what had gone before or doubts about what might lay ahead.

She had to look up, she had to! She couldn't go on looking at her plate, but the knowledge that Jay was still studying her kept her eyes riveted to it. Mike saved her, coming in with a plate that was even fuller than her own and putting it in front of Jay.

'Thanks!' Jay spoke and Dulcie risked a glance to find that he was looking up at the smiling

Indian boy. 'Where's Lori, do you know?'

'Out in the yard.' Mike jerked his head in the general direction of the back of the house. 'Fixing the grass. I've been giving her a hand,' he added, explaining his dirty boots and fingernails.

'You'll leave her alone!' The terseness in Jay's voice wiped the smile from Mike's face. 'When I give an order around here, I want it carried out. Lori caused the damage and she'll make it good herself—understand?'

'Yes, boss.'

So much for equality at Rose Valley Ranch, Dulcie thought, as Mike's face crumpled. Jay might be wearing a shirt and a pair of faded jeans, just like the boy, and he might also have the same hard, untamed quality that Lloyd Southwind had, but he also had authority—it was stamped in every inch of him—and equality began and ended at Rose Valley just where Jay Maitland said it would. Forgetting her earlier selfconsciousness, Dulcie began to seethe.

'And tell Lori I expect her indoors, cleaned up and ready to start work in ten minutes,' Jay added.

'Yes, boss!' Mike almost crept out of the room.

Don't say anything! *Don't* say anything! Dulcie warned herself, but it was still her voice that she heard speaking out. 'Weren't you a little hard on him?' she asked.

Jay shot her a non-committal glance. 'Why?'

'Well, Mike's obviously fond of Lori,' Dulcie began to falter under the pressure of his stare.

'It's good for her to have a friend near her own age and if he wants to help her—well, maybe I could help him with the work around the house . . . to compensate,' she added lamely.

Jay said nothing and went back to his steak and there was a long silence before the mane of blond hair finally lifted and the grey eyes drilled into her once more.

'You,' he said, 'are here for a specific reason, and that doesn't include keeping house. That's Mike's job and he'll do it. Yours is to inject a little feminine example into my daughter's life, and now, perhaps, is the moment to explain exactly what that does—and does not—mean.'

It was also the moment when she should have spoken out; refused to stay and demanded that he make arrangements to have her flown to Winnipeg so that she could catch the next flight home, but the tongue that had provoked his scathing outburst now refused to work.

'Firstly,' he said flatly, 'you will not undermine my authority in my house. Secondly, you will fit yourself into our routine. I tutor Lori here and she'll go on doing lessons with me every morning. The rest of the day you may spend with her as you wish.'

'*You* tutor her?' Dulcie could not help the note of surprise that crept into her voice.

'You find that difficult to believe?' If she had not known that it was impossible, Dulcie could have sworn that a hint of amusement had crept into the steel-grey eyes. 'I have a university degree and I also run a multi-million-dollar agri-cultural business—and make no mistake, that's what farming on a grand scale is these days—a business! Don't you think that qualifies me to tutor a twelve-year-old child, or do you still think I'm incompetent?'

'Well, yes . . . no . . . I mean,' Dulcie stumbled badly. That wasn't what she had meant and he knew it.

'In spite of anything you may have assumed,' he said, 'I love my daughter and I want what's best for her. Although she may have had the mis-fortune to have been born an embryonic woman, I have no intention of allowing her to grow up ignorant!' Now there was no mistaking the barbed humour. 'She has a fine brain and I expect her to go on to university and then on into a career.'

'But I thought you were against women having a career?' Dulcie just did not understand.

'I'm against anyone—man or woman—making an emotional commitment and then sacrificing it for the sake of a career,' he said quietly. 'It hap-pened to me and to Lori. She's too young to re-member, but I can.'

At first Dulcie thought he was talking about his wife, but as he went on, she realised he was talking about his own childhood.

'My father gave us everything we could want. A home,' he glanced around the fine old furniture in the dusty room, 'security even, when he'd paid off the last mortgage on the ranch. He gave us everything except his time, his interest and his love.' He looked away, back into distant time. 'They all went elsewhere. He left my mother a year before he died. She never quite recovered.'

'And so you're going to make sure that your daughter will never be foolish enough to fall in love!' Dulcie seethed at the injustice that visited the experience of the father on the child.

'I'm trying to make sure she'll grow up strong enough to be able to overcome whatever disappointments life has in store,' Jay corrected her. 'I accept the fact that one day she'll be a woman and that I'm not equipped to teach her how to handle that!' His eyes snapped back into focus. 'That's your job,' he finished abruptly. 'That's why you're here.'

'To teach Lori how to be a docile and obedient member of the weaker sex!' Dulcie accused.

'If that's how you choose to see it—yes!' The other thoughts chasing across the surface of his face were not put into words. 'You're here for Lori's sake—and nothing else!'

It was an impossible situation and one in which she would be a fool to stay, but Dulcie knew that she was not going to leave when she stood at her bedroom window a short while later and gazed out at the partially repaired tyre tracks across the damaged lawn.

Lori needed her. In spite of the fact that when she had come into the dining room, she had gone to stand beside her father, two against one, daring Dulcie to come between them, Lori needed her as much as any of the children with whom she had worked in London.

But if Lori's resentment was understandable, Jay's was much more difficult to comprehend. He might not have welcomed the idea, but he had asked her to come to Rose Valley—the letter in her bag was proof of that—and yet from the moment she had arrived he had seemed set on doing his best to make her turn tail and leave.

His bitterness intrigued her. It ran through everything like the currents in a pool, so close to the surface and so alive that the wounds of his father's lack of interest and his wife's desertion might have been inflicted only yesterday. Surely in all the years that had followed, some emotional scar tissue should have begun to form. If it wasn't such a fantastic notion, she might have thought that he was cherishing his bitterness as a defence against the dangerous trap of ever giving his love to anyone again.

Rubbish! Dulcie shook her head and the lawn outside her window disappeared behind a flying pinwheel of silky dark red hair. Although she might not be able to ignore the feelings of arousal and alarm Jay had stirred in her from the moment they had met in London four thousand miles away, she must never, ever, allow herself to imagine that his response could in any way match hers.

Besides, she was going to marry Ross. After this brief time out from her normal life, she was going home to him. And even if she wasn't, as far as Jay was concerned, she was no more than an unwelcome intruder, briefly and reluctantly allowed into his life for the benefit of his daughter. He had spelled that out; she could still hear the certainty in his voice. What more did she need to tell her that, if it had been entirely up to Jay, she would not be there?

And, rather than spend the morning in her room trying to analyse these dangerous waves of fantasy, she would be wiser to spend her time taking her first look at the ranch.

The name might be Rose Valley, but there was not a rose in sight, even though it was mid-June and the gardens in England would be full of them. Instead, there were just prairie lilies, planted at intervals on the lawn, blindingly orange against the white walls of the house and reflecting the sun in a dazzling glare from which there was no escape; not in the brilliant green of the watered lawn where slowly turning sprinklers were making rainbows in the sun nor in the brilliant aquamarine of the pool, its colour intensified and doubled by the even more vivid blue of an immense and cloudless prairie sky.

She began to walk around the back of the house, passing her bedroom window and cutting across the grass when the path stopped. Barns and paddocks lay ahead of her, empty except for a few horses dozing in the shade, and there wasn't a soul in sight but, beyond the barns, there was another house—a much older one.

Dulcie looked at it, intrigued. It was right at

the back and in the centre of the windbreak. The bungalow was much further forward and much less protected, but this house looked as if it had had the trees planted especially to give it their protection and she started to walk towards it, screwing up her eyes against the glare.

It seemed to be two stories high, built of mellow brick with dormer windows in the black-tiled roof and a carved wooden verandah running along the front, with the pattern of the verandah repeated in the decorative barge board on the roof. It was also inhabited, she realised when she got closer and saw the outline of furniture behind the wire mesh screens in the open windows.

'Do you wanna tell me where you're going?' A pair of scuffed cowboy boots came into her field of vision on the top of the verandah steps and Dulcie looked up to see Lloyd Southwind towering over her.

'I thought I'd take a look around the ranch. Mr Maitland—Jay—said it would be all right.' Although she knew she had no need to justify herself to Jay's foreman when Jay had made it more than clear that she could go anywhere and do anything with her morning except interrupt him and Lori at their lessons, Dulcie suddenly felt an overwhelming need to gain approval—anyone's approval. But if she had expected it from Lloyd, she was disappointed when the tall Indian came down the steps.

'Did Jay tell you to come over here?' he asked sharply.

His fierceness puzzled her. 'No.'

'Then keep away!' he said. 'This is the bunk-house—the hired hands live here. Men!' he added to make absolutely sure she understood.

Of all the . . .! Lloyd had already made it clear on their flight from Winnipeg that he was just as unenthusiastic as his employer about having a woman on the ranch, but if he thought her main reason for coming was because she would be the only woman with a lot of men, then she had better set him straight.

Before she could start, Lloyd had punctured her bubble of furious indignation with an explanation. 'Some of the characters living here I'd trust,' he said, 'and some of 'em I wouldn't! Not with a woman, anyways—or with much else, come to that. They're mostly saddle bums and drifters, just passing through. Best keep away from here, ma'am.'

He was walking her back to the bungalow as they talked and Dulcie felt extremely foolish. 'Oh, I see!' she said. 'But whose house was it, though?' she asked as he seemed disposed to talk.

'Jay's grandpa's. He built it when he settled hereabouts. Jay moved out of it a while ago.'

'Why did Jay move out?' Dulcie thought it strange that anyone should give up this pleasant old house with all its character and charm in favour of the much more impersonal bungalow.

'He'll tell you that himself, I guess, if he's a mind.' Lloyd glanced down at her. 'Didn't anyone tell you to get yourself a hat?'

'A hat?' Completely taken aback by the sudden switch in conversation, Dulcie put her hand up to her head and was surprised to find it was quite hot. The breeze, she supposed, had stopped her realising it. 'No,' she said.

'Then we'd best find you one.' They were back in front of the bungalow and, apparently taking it for granted that she would follow, Lloyd went inside and when Dulcie caught up with him, he was rummaging in one of the untidy cupboards in the hall. Would she ever get used to the offhand way these men treated women? she wondered as she stood and watched him.

'Here, this should do.' Lloyd banged the dust out of a cream stetson and held it out.

It fitted perfectly, and as she adjusted it on her chestnut curls, Dulcie knew instinctively whose hat it was.

'Did you know Jay's wife?' It was the last question she had intended to ask and it also came out much too quickly for her peace of mind, but to her surprise, Lloyd not only took it in his stride, but looked at her with the beginnings of a smile, the first she had seen since he had met her at the airport.

'Valerie? Sure did. But don't worry,' he said wryly, 'you ain't nothin' like her. And the hat ain't hers, neither, if that's what's botherin' you,' he added as he walked away.

If Dulcie hadn't been so mortified by the ease with which she had given herself away, she might have stopped to wonder to whom the hat did belong if it was not to Jay's ex-wife, but as it was, she was more intrigued with the name she had just learned.

Valerie. She turned it over experimentally in her mind. It had associations with someone cool and self-possessed—someone much more like a Dorothea than a Dulcie. Beautiful, too, if she had left her husband and her baby daughter to go to Hollywood, although Dulcie had never heard of a film star called Valerie Maitland and the name certainly seemed good enough to use professionally. Perhaps Jay had objected or perhaps, to make the break complete, Valerie had reverted to her maiden name or had chosen a completely different one. It was hardly likely that she would ever find out; Jay was certainly the last person she could ask.

The only thing she knew—and was ever likely to know—was what Lloyd had told her: that Valerie Maitland wasn't in the least like her. In which case, she was probably tall, dark and beautiful with the near-black hair that she had passed on to her daughter. She certainly wouldn't be small and fair-skinned with a mop of curls that, two shades lighter, would have been plain carrot.

Dulcie shook her curls. Different or not, the notion of wearing the hat she held in her hand was suddenly distasteful. Or perhaps it was that she was tired; still not over the jet lag of her journey the day before. Either way, the idea of spending what was left of the morning lazing in the

garden swing at the end of the pool suddenly
became infinitely more appealing than setting out
on another solitary walk around the ranch.

She would put that off until later, when it was
cooler. Also, perhaps asking Lori to show her
round would be a good way of breaking the ice—
Dulcie smiled at the small pun—especially as it
was anything but icy as she picked her way across
the tiled surround of the pool towards the refuge
of the swing at the far end.

The swing was shady under its floral canopy
and her weight set up a motion that created a
small breeze. She relaxed back with a sigh, careful to keep out of the direct light of the sun. She
burned and freckled easily, and one of the first
things she must do was ask if there was a town
nearby where she could buy some sun tan
lotion—and a hat!

It didn't seem likely, though. The prairie
seemed to go on for ever when she looked out
over the back of the swing. She could see some
cattle grazing in the shade of scrub that was more
than bushes but less than trees, but there was
nothing else. The nearest town could be a million
miles away, but the pool was closer and much
more tempting.

Although she had not expected there to be the
luxury of a pool, she had at least brought her
bikini, and she looked down at the minute scraps
of black lycra, stark against the whiteness of her
skin. The bikini had been Ross's choice, not
something she would have chosen for herself,

but, by the end of their holiday in Spain the previous year, wearing just one bikini amid the thousands on the beach, she had lost her selfconsciousness about what she had originally considered her near-nudity.

She looked at the pool again and the temptation was too strong. There was no one about, so Jay could hardly accuse her of flaunting herself in front of the hired hands, and if she kept as much of herself as possible underneath the surface of the water and put on her wrap the moment she came out, she shouldn't burn. Without pausing to think about it any more, she ran across the hot tiles and dived in.

The water was too beautiful to leave. Just one more length and then she would get out and go indoors and dress for lunch. Dulcie slipped into the rhythm of a long, even crawl, revelling in the use of unused muscles as she stroked the length of the full-sized pool and feeling her hair lengthening and straightening in the water until it clung smoothly and darkly around her head and streamed back across her shoulders.

Swimming was something she did well. It was a joy, a complete relaxation, clearing her mind of everything except the sheer physical sensation of another element against her skin. She got to the end beside the diving board and broke the surface in a spray of iridescent drops, aware of the immediate heat of the sun upon her face. Just once more down and back!

She was half way back to her wrap on the

swing beside the diving board when the water in front of her exploded in a cloud of bubbles and she surfaced in Jay's arms.

'I see you've found a way of keeping yourself amused!' He was smiling, playful even, certainly more relaxed than she had seen him since she had arrived, and there was nothing in his face or voice to put her on her guard. It was his body that did that—warm, in spite of the comparative coolness of the pool, virile and so close that she could feel her own near nudity responding in a way that terrified her.

Mesmerised by the sensation he had aroused, she hung there for a second, her fingers tangled in his mane of hair and her face on a level with his smile and with the sunlight and amusement dancing in his eyes.

Appalled, she dropped her hands, but the treacherous pressure of the water would not let her go. Instead, it pushed her closer to him, brushing the hardness of his thighs and stomach and making her conscious of his sudden muscular response to her unwilling provocation.

Her own response, however, was far more dangerous, and in a fit of mounting panic that had nothing to do with drowning, she struggled free of his arms.

When she surfaced, she was several yards away, but not so far that she couldn't see that his eyes had lost their humour and that his smile had changed into a cynical, twisted line. It was quite clear that he thought she had been provoking him, and her best defence—not just against him but against the turbulent arousal he had created—was attack.

'How dare you do that?' she blazed, charging her residual passion with the spark of anger.

'How dare I do what?' he questioned her. 'Use my own pool for my regular lunchtime swim?'

'No, I mean, how dare you. . . .' Dulcie stopped abruptly, caught in a trap she had set herself. If she went on to explain why she was so outraged, she would be leaving herself open to an accusation that was partially true. That she had delayed her escape seconds longer than she need have, deliberately turning a playful encounter into one of mutual sexual arousal.

'How dare you dive in and frighten me like that!' she substituted lamely, looking quickly away as the colour began to flood her cheeks.

'Scare you?' The lack of credence in his voice brought her eyes swiftly back to find him smiling in a way that made her suddenly afraid. With his mane of hair flattened and darkened by the water and his teeth glinting in the sun, he no longer reminded her of a prairie lion but of a wolf, studying a weaker prey that had been foolish enough to tempt him.

'Having spent the last few minutes watching you, I hardly think a fear of drowning is what you're talking about. You swim much too well to be afraid of that!' He spoke quite conversationally, but before she had a chance to guess what he intended, he had launched himself forward, cutting through the water with a powerful ease and reaching her before she had a chance to swim away.

'Let's see what else you do well, shall we?' He bit the words out close beside her ear, but then his mouth had moved to cover hers.

At first she fought, struggling against herself as well as him and bruising her mouth as she wrenched her head savagely back and forth until his hands slid down her spine, turning her skin to satin in the water, and she felt herself responding with a terrifying force.

The moment she surrendered Jay let her go, pushing her from him with a strength that left her bikini top in his fingers, and she went underneath the surface in a swirl of water. When she finally came up, dazed and bemused by the frightening power of her response and his rejection, he was pulling himself out of the pool with one lithe, sinuous movement, water streaming from his powerful back and shoulders, apparently naked in his brief bathing trunks.

He turned and held out his hand, bronzed and supremely masculine against a background of the brilliant sunshine. 'Here!'

'I can't!' She looked pleadingly at the scrap of black lycra he had dropped on the tiled surround.

'Haven't you left it a little late to be so modest?' Ignoring the top of her bikini, he suddenly bent and caught both her hands in his, lifting her from the pool and lowering her slowly and deliberately along the full length of his body before her feet touched the ground. 'Now,' he said, 'put on your wrap. The men are coming in for the noon hour break.'

CHAPTER FOUR

GOING into the dining room and facing Jay over lunch was the hardest thing Dulcie had ever done in her life. His face gave away nothing of what he might be thinking and he barely spoke to her, concentrating most of his attention on Lori, but just the fact that he was there was enough to bring her to the screaming pitch of self-awareness.

And it was so ironic. It had always troubled her that she had never felt the slightest hint of passionate arousal whenever Ross had taken her in his arms, and now she had and she was wishing with all her heart that she had not.

Just the sound of Jay's voice was enough to make her breath catch in her throat, and when she risked a glance in his direction and saw his hair, still damp and darkened like her own, her whole body burned in a way that had nothing to do with too much exposure to the sun.

How dared he take advantage of her like that! Dulcie tried swamping her new-found and frightening physical awareness with an anger that she knew was feigned. Just as she knew that it was her fault as much as his that those few minutes in the pool had taken place. No—more!

If she hadn't hung there in his arms until the pressure of the water had pushed her half naked body so intimately close, Jay would never have mistaken her hesitation for invitation and she wouldn't be sitting in this neglected room more conscious of him than she had ever been of any man in her life.

It had been the water that had kept her in his arms, but it hadn't been the water that had created her reaction, and the only thing she could do now to try and regain at least a measure of her self-respect was to make sure that nothing remotely like it ever happened again.

But what if she didn't get the chance? A void formed in the pit of her stomach. Jay had never made any attempt to hide the fact that it had been Gerry's insistence that had brought her to Rose Valley. Jay had never wanted her there—and that had been before she had apparently flung herself at him in the most blatant way.

What if, now that she had confirmed all his worst suspicions about women, he took her on one side when this interminable lunch was over, and suggested that she leave on the grounds that she was the last person he wanted as an example for his daughter?

The stab of anguish this idea created was enough to make her forget she was holding a fork and it clattered down on to her plate, drawing Jay's eyes in a brief, incurious glance. How strange life was! Only this morning she had been the one who had been thinking of insisting that he make arrangements to have her flown back to Winnipeg. Now all she wanted was to be allowed to stay.

'But Dad, I planned to go out on my bike this afternoon!' Lori's voice rose resentfully and Dulcie's ears tuned into a conversation that had been going on without her hearing it. 'I promised Mike. . . .'

'Then you'll have to tell Mike that you've got to break your promise,' Jay cut in. 'I want him to help with the round-up anyway. You'll do your homework in your room and then you'll show Dulcie round the ranch.'

'But, Dad . . .!' Lori started up again.

'That's enough!' Jay's voice cracked across her. 'You'll show Dulcie round and that's an order!' He stood, blocking the light from the window with his back to Lori and facing Dulcie. 'That way, maybe, you can both keep each other out of mischief—and on dry land!'

He couldn't be teasing, he just couldn't! If his anger and desire to punish had really faded and if he was really looking at her as if sharing the secret of their encounter in the pool with some amusement, he would be talking about showing her around the ranch himself. He wouldn't be making arrangements on her behalf as if she was some unwelcome encumbrance that he wanted safely out of the way for a few hours.

'By the way,' he glanced back at Lori from the doorway, 'you're not to ride that bike of yours again until I give permission. You've done quite enough damage with it for a while.'

'Hell!' Lori waited to relieve her feelings until even the echo of Jay's footsteps had died away, but even so, she was careful to speak quietly in case some sixth sense might bring him back again.

Dulcie carefully looked down at her plate. It was still too soon to take Lori to task for language, and besides, Lori did have some justification. Jay's open-ended punishment was too harsh for what appeared to have been no more than a spur-of-the-moment impulse to work off her feelings about Dulcie's arrival on the inoffensive grass, and Jay shouldn't have left her without knowing when she could have her treasured motorcycle back.

Dulcie smiled at the plate in front of her, still loaded with the remains of her scarcely touched lunch. It had been so easy to slip back into her professional role and start thinking about the often unintended effects of parental punishment on children that she had quite forgotten how much, in this case, both parent and child resented her.

She smiled again and, for some inconsequential reason, felt much better.

'What are you grinning about?' Lori scraped her chair back and stood looking at Dulcie, taut and angry with a lock of curly black hair falling across her forehead. 'I shouldn't be surprised if you put him up to it!' she snapped.

'Put who up to what?' Dulcie asked carefully.

'Getting Dad to take my motorcycle away!' She pronounced the word cycle to rhyme with fickle but even with the difference in pronunciation, the meaning was absolutely clear. Lori felt that she had been unjustly treated and that she was looking at the cause. 'You're here to show me how to be a lady, aren't you?' Lori went on passionately. 'And ladies don't ride dirt bikes!'

Dulcie ignored the gibe. 'I don't think your father means to take it away completely,' she said reasonably. 'Maybe when you've calmed down a bit, you should go and ask him when you can have it back.'

Lori studied her; dark where he was fair but otherwise so like him that Dulcie's heart gave a little flip. 'You think he'd tell me?' she said eventually.

'It wouldn't hurt to ask.'

The dark eyes didn't waver, but the angry tension bottled up in the taut little body in its cotton top and jeans visibly started to relax. 'Wouldn't you mind?'

'No, why should I?' Dulcie was genuinely bewildered by the question.

'Because ladies don't ride dirt bikes and you're here to turn me into a lady, like I said.' Lori smiled. For the first time she actually smiled, and for the first time since she had arrived at Rose Valley, Dulcie saw a gleam of hope in the relationship that had been thrust upon them both, but it was a gleam that was promptly extinguished later that afternoon when Lori obeyed her father's instructions to show Dulcie around the ranch.

The first part of the afternoon dragged interminably. Alone in her room, Dulcie heard sounds that she supposed meant that the men, with Jay among them, were riding off to round up the cattle, but then there was complete, unbroken silence. She started to write letters, but the one to Ross was hard to finish and she finally gave up, glancing at her watch and wondering if Lori had had a change of heart and given her the slip. Perhaps she ought to go and look for her. Jay's room, she knew, was at the end of the long passage where all the bedrooms were, but Lori's was one or two along from hers. But which one was it? she thought blankly, looking at the series of closed doors. She knocked on the first one. There was no reply, but Lori could possibly be sulking. Perhaps she should look. She turned the knob and stopped in stunned surprise.

She was looking at a woman's room with rose pink curtains, a matching carpet and a softly draped and canopied bed, but it was more than that that kept her rooted to the spot. It was the faint hint of perfume in the air and a feeling that the room was still in use. But how could that be? There hadn't been a woman living at Rose Valley for twelve years.

'What are you doing?' The voice startled her. It was hard and taut, just like Jay's. 'You shouldn't be in there, that's *her* room!'

Lori had come up behind her with a face like a thundercloud. She must mean that the room had been her mother's, though why Jay and his wife should have had separate rooms was more than Dulcie could fathom. It was also strange that the room should have been kept in such good order—almost like a shrine. As Jay obviously despised his ex-wife so much, it would have been much more natural for him to have got rid of every trace of her. But then she had already discovered how illogical Jay could be—hostile to the point of open warfare one minute, and teasing and conciliatory the next.

'Do you want me to show you round or not?' Lori was already turning away, and Dulcie shrugged off her uncomfortable intuition about the room and followed her.

The lunchtime smile that she had hoped might mark the start of a turning point in their relationship was no more than a memory on Lori's hostile face as she showed her round, and, apart from the strangeness of her surroundings and the immensity of the prairie surrounding the tiny patch of civilisation that was the ranch, Dulcie found there wasn't much to see.

The stock was out at grass and they went through barns stacked to the rafters with hay and others housing huge pieces of agricultural equipment. There were three cars in one—a Porsche, a Cadillac and a Rolls—but none of them looked as if they had nearly as much use as a battered jeep parked in a far corner.

'Rich man, poor man!' A remark Gerry had made in London began to make more sense. Jay could afford anything he wanted—except happiness.

The smell of hay drifting towards them on the rising breeze highlighted Lori's attitude of chilly indifference when they went outside.

'Do you like living here?' After what seemed an eternity of standing with their elbows hooked over the top rail of a corral fence watching a group of horses dozing in the shade, Dulcie tried to break the heavy silence. Getting no reply, she tried again. 'What would you like to do when you grow up?'

Lori didn't turn her head. 'Be like Mike!' she said shortly.

'Mike?' It was the last answer Dulcie would have expected. 'You mean to say you'd like to keep house?'

'Of course not!' Lori favoured her with a contemptuous glance. 'I want to be an engineer. That's what Mike's going to be.'

'An engineer?'

Lori sighed. How could anyone be so stupid? 'Dad's putting him through college,' she said patiently. 'He starts in the fall. Dad says everyone deserves a chance to make the best of themselves if they've got guts and potential,' she spoke the words clearly, obviously quoting. 'That's why he paid for Lloyd to get his pilot's licence. Lloyd could have his own business crop spraying now, if he wanted, but he likes it here with us.'

So that explained Lloyd's fierce loyalty. It also disclosed a side of Jay that Dulcie would never have dreamed existed.

'But Mike'll have to go and live somewhere

else if he wants to be an engineer, won't he?'

A shutter came down over Lori's eyes. 'I guess so.' She hid her feelings with an indifferent shrug. 'Dad'll just have to get someone else to take care of us, that's all.'

Someone with guts and potential, Dulcie thought, and someone who didn't have the over-whelming disadvantage of being a woman!

'Do you want to go for a ride?' Lori had stopped staring at the horses and was looking at Dulcie with something like enthusiasm on her previously frigid face.

'I don't know.' Dulcie was doubtful. It was a step forward, and yet there was something behind the expression in the dark eyes watching her that wasn't as straightforward as it seemed. 'I haven't ridden since I was a child,' she added.

'You're scared!' Lori was immediately con-temptuous.

'No, not scared—just a bit too old!' Dulcie tried a laugh, but Lori was unimpressed.

'My dad's thirty-five,' she said, 'and he's not scared of any horse!' She ducked underneath the rail and headed towards the horses.

There was no doubt she was a shrewd psy-chologist. Even though a sixth sense told her Jay would not approve, Dulcie knew she could not refuse to go. It hardly seemed possible that things between her and Lori could get better, but they could certainly get worse, and if Jay could call the experiment a failure, he would lose no time in telling her to leave.

Catching hold of the brim of her hat, Dulcie ducked underneath the rail. The complete cowgirl in her cowboy hat and jeans—the complete cowgirl in everything but courage!

The horses scattered as she approached them and she stepped quickly back.

'It's okay, they won't hurt you.' Lori smiled and sounded reassuring. 'You'd better have old Bowler. You're a bit alike.'

Dulcie studied the fat brown and white pony Lori was saddling but could see no resemblance. What she could see, however, was the expression on Lori's face when she came up from under the pony's belly holding the buckle end of the leather girth. Lori was pleased; she was actually pleased! What a fool she would have been to have given in to her misgivings about what Jay might say. This ride could mark a real turning point.

After taking infinite pains to adjust the stirrups to Dulcie's legs and make sure she was comfortable, Lori quickly saddled and mounted a frisky black and led the way out of the corral. Bowler went quietly. He bowled along, in fact, Dulcie thought happily, beginning to enjoy herself and scarcely noticing when the pony broke into an easy trot. Riding had never particularly interested her, but it was easier than she remembered as a child, particularly in this high Western saddle with the saddle horn to hold on to if she felt insecure.

'Are you okay?'

'Fine! What's that over there?' Dulcie bravely

took one hand from the reins and pointed to a
moving cloud of dust that she had been watching
blowing in from the horizon on the increasingly
gusty wind. No, it must be closer than that. She
could see the hazy line of the horizon behind the
dust and the cloud was getting closer.

Lori's reply was lost in a curious drumming
noise, overlaid with the sound of men shouting
and cracking whips and getting louder all the
time, and Dulcie had a fleeting impression of
cattle and horses in the blowing dust before
Bowler suddenly changed from a trot to a flat-out
gallop and began to take her straight towards the
centre of a herd being driven back towards the
ranch.

The pony neither swerved nor tried to throw
her but just galloped straight ahead. For a second
there was a chance as Lori desperately tried to
intercept them, but then they were past and
Dulcie was sitting terrified, wedged in the high
saddle which had once seemed comfortingly like
an armchair but now seemed like a trap, watching
the wicked points of a thousand long, curved
horns rushing up towards them.

There was nothing she could do to save herself.
The first steers scattered as Bowler charged into
them, a pair of horns missing her thigh by inches
as a furiously bellowing Hereford turned away,
but then they were in the middle of the herd and
the dust was rising in blinding waves, clogging
her nostrils with the pungent, overpowering
smell of cattle. The noise was deafening, no

longer coming through her ears but pounding inside her head and vibrating through her body as she fought to keep her balance in a saddle that had turned into glass. Bowler swerved and she knew that if he swerved again she would fall, and there would be nothing she could do to save herself from being trampled beneath the milling hooves.

Suddenly they were through. It was not her eyes that told her, but her ears, gradually regaining their ability to separate and distinguish sound so that the noise of the stampeding cattle no longer seemed to be coming from inside her head but was more distant and overlaid with the sounds of Bowler's galloping hooves and of another horse coming up fast behind them.

Spurred on by the pursuit, she could feel Bowler stretch his muscles in a supreme effort, but, a second later, the dim outline of a buckskin stallion, blurred by dust and stinging tears, was overtaking them at a gallop and a hand caught hold of Bowler's reins and brought him to a neighing, skidding halt. An arm went round her waist and Dulcie felt herself lifted bodily from the saddle.

'What the hell do you think you're doing? Trying to kill yourself?' The voice vibrated through her skull, as hard and abrasive as the tough denim shirt beneath her cheek and as strong as the heart beating against her breast. 'Can't you be trusted to keep out of trouble for a second?'

'I'm sorry!' It was woefully and pitifully inadequate, but Dulcie could think of nothing else to say as she looked up past the tanned skin exposed by the shirt and past the corded column of his neck into the thunderously angry expression on Jay's face.

'Okay, now whose idea was it to ride out to the herd?' Jay looked from one to the other of them, no longer furiously angry but hard and cold in a way that was much more frightening. Lori dropped her head and Dulcie forced herself to face the steely eyes boring into her.

'Mine,' she said, beginning a long silence she thought would never end.

They were back home in the hall-cum-living room of the ranch, still in their sweat and dirt-streaked clothes. Jay had taken off his hat and was standing facing them, a lean, whipcord figure in the denim shirt and jeans that had done nothing to make Dulcie less aware of the flesh and bone and muscle under them on the ride back to the ranch.

Instead of putting her back on Bowler, Jay had curtly told one of the boys to catch the pony and lead him home. He had kept Dulcie on his horse with him, shifting his weight to give her room between his thighs and the saddlehorn. With his arm brushing the soft curve of her breast, the terror of her mad dash into the herd had gradually given way to a supreme physical awareness, and when he had finally reined in in the yard and Lloyd had helped her down, her sense of loss at leaving him was as acute as any pain.

Jay's thoughts at the conclusion of what, if it had not been so fantastic, she might have believed had been the contrived intimacy of their ride were, however, a mystery, and there had been only anger in his voice when he had called for Lori to follow them and walked with her back into the house.

'So it was your idea to ride out to the herd, was it?' The voice of the man who filled her thoughts cut through the tension-laden atmosphere in the hall and brought her back to the present with a jolt.

She glanced at Lori, but Lori was studying her toes. 'Yes,' she said.

It was wrong, she knew, to take the blame. Everything she had ever read during her training and everything she had had to do with children at the clinic in London had convinced her that honesty was the only way. However good her motives, now that Lori had heard her lying she would probably never trust her word again. Her only excuse was that as she was now hardly likely to be staying at Rose Valley long enough for it to matter, she might just as well take the blame and save Lori from another dose of her father's heavy-handed punishment.

'And I suppose it was also your idea to ride Bowler?' Jay went on.

'That's right!' Dulcie threw all sense of preservation to the winds. 'He looked so quiet and fat, you see,' she added, realising that some explanation was needed for her insistence on one particular horse above the others when she knew none of them and had been at Rose Valley only slightly more than twenty-four hours. Twenty-four hours! So much had happened in that small space of time that it seemed more like a lifetime.

'In that case, I think you should go to your room.' Jay looked meaningfully at his daughter. 'Dulcie and I need to have a little talk.'

It was the first time he had ever used her name and, in her quick involuntary response, Dulcie almost missed the look of apology mixed with pleading that Lori shot in her direction as she left.

'Would you like a drink?' Jay opened a glass-fronted cupboard and produced two mismatched crystal tumblers. 'Mike! Ice!' he called, getting out a bottle of rye whisky.

'No ... yes ... I mean, I don't know.' Why should the sound of her name on his lips make her so suddenly confused? She had heard it a million times before, but never with quite that purring edge that proved a shiver really could run down your spine.

'If you're not certain, I suggest you say yes.' Jay poured a full measure of rye into the second glass. 'I've a feeling you're not going to like what I have to say.'

The void that had opened up earlier that day in her stomach opened up again. He was about to tell her that she should leave Rose Valley and there was nothing she could do about it, any more than there had been anything she could do about the terrifying certainty of being trampled to death when Bowler had taken her into the middle of the herd.

'Here you are, boss!' Her sentence was postponed as Mike appeared with a battered enamel bowl of ice cubes which he put down on a beautifully carved rosewood table. 'Supper in an hour, is that okay?' he asked before he left.

'What? Yes, that's fine.' Jay suddenly seemed as preoccupied as Dulcie was herself.

What was happening to her? she thought, aware of her quick intake of breath as Jay's fingers brushed hers as he handed her her drink. She had been under his roof for little more than a day, and in that time he had done nothing to dispel her original impression that she was there against his will. How then could she possibly be so appalled at the thought of being sent away?

'Sit down!' Jay pointed to the couch and Dulcie sat, moving into the corner as she felt him sit at the other end.

'I know you were lying about what happened earlier,' he said abruptly. 'What I want to know is why.'

Entirely taken by surprise, Dulcie felt the colour flooding to her cheeks.

'How do you know?' she asked lamely, struggling for time.

'Because Bowler is a rogue horse. He's un-predictable. We don't use him for visitors.' He paused. 'Now tell me it was your idea to ride him and not Lori's.'

Surely Lori hadn't deliberately tried to get her killed? The thought drove home how hopeless her situation was, but Jay misread her sudden appalled silence.

'Oh, come now,' he jeered. 'Save me the pre-varication! I had at least credited you with honesty, but I can see I was wrong. Like most women, you probably don't know how to tell the truth!' He watched her with contempt.

This was too much! Dulcie suddenly stopped worrying about being asked to leave and began to fume with total anger. If this—she stumbled in her mind to find the right word—if this auto-cratic, insufferable and totally wrong-headed man wanted the truth, then he should have it.

'I took the blame because I think you're much too hard on Lori,' she said bluntly. 'I think you over-react when she does anything wrong and I also think that if you go on punishing her as harshly as you do, you'll end up alienating her and driving her away.'

Just as you probably drove your wife away, she thought, but didn't say it.

There was a moment's absolute silence as he studied her, a myriad swiftly changing emotions crossing the shadowed surface of his face, but any faint hope that he might show some understand-ing crumbled under the cutting edge of his voice.

'The next time you decide to shield my daughter,' he said harshly, 'remember that you're here to provide her with an appropriate female model, not to teach her how to lie!'

CHAPTER FIVE

THE injustice of Jay's allegation sent Dulcie
speechless from the room, and the wave of anger
it created kept returning to engulf her over the
next few days. Sometimes she would think it had
subsided, at least to the point where she could
view her situation rationally and with a measure
of her old professional calm—after all, some of
the parents of the children she had seen at the
clinic in London had said worse things to her
than that!—but then some quirk of inner chem-
istry would set her turning the whole incident
over in her mind and she would find herself
burning with sheer frustrated humiliation and
outright rage.

How dared he speak to her like that! Especially
when all she had been doing was trying to stop
him from driving Lori away. But perhaps that
was what he wanted! Perhaps his wife's desertion
had left him so disillusioned about women that he
would even sacrifice his daughter to prove his
point.

At times her frustration about the impossibility
of the job she had been sent to do brought Dulcie
to the verge of packing her things and demanding
to go home.

But what was the point? she asked herself one night when thought had given way to action and she had her suitcases open and already half packed on her bed. Jay would doubtless refuse to let Lloyd fly her back to Winnipeg until it suited him, and the prospect of having to stay on, waiting for his permission and knowing that he was very probably amused by her admission of defeat, was more than she could tolerate.

And flying to Winnipeg was the only way. She knew now how far the ranch was from the nearest railway station.

She tipped the clothes she had put into her suitcases out on to the bed and started to put them away again in the built-in wardrobe and chest of drawers in her room.

It had taken an hour that afternoon to drive to Rose Town—a village, in spite of the promise of its name—and that had been at the speed at which Jay drove. And although Rose Town had a railway, it was only a branch line, used exclusively for shipping grain; Jay had told her that when he had noticed her looking at the wagons with their romantic names. Canadian Pacific, Sioux, Hudson Bay—names from all over the North American continent, reminding her just how far she was from home as she stood there in the little prairie town looking at the wagons stretching back along the tracks from the grain elevators for as far as she could see.

It was almost, she thought later, as if Jay had guessed what she had been thinking—that the train had given her the wild idea of getting a taxi into Rose Town and going on by rail to Winnipeg.

But that was probably as wrong as her impression that the disappearance of Jay's wedding ring had any real significance.

She had noticed that he was no longer wearing it on the drive back. Even though Lori had been with them, she was buried in a comic book in the back and the atmosphere had been tense and strained, the miles passing with no one saying anything.

At one point Dulcie had been studying Jay, unable to stop her eyes drifting over his hard profile and thinking how well the harsh demanding land in which he had chosen to make his life suited his personality, when he had glanced across and she had immediately looked down.

At first she had looked without seeing, but then she realised that the hand on the steering wheel was completely bare, with only a faint white mark against the tanned skin to show where his wedding ring had been. She checked. It was certainly his ring finger and the white band was proof that she wasn't wrong. He *had* been wearing a ring in London. Why then had he chosen to take it off now when he was at home? What had made him finally decide to remove the last outward symbol of his marriage?

The little mystery had puzzled her, but now she shook her head and went mechanically on with putting away the clothes she had tipped out on to the bed.

Jay Maitland was a law unto himself. He was answerable to no one for his actions, and if she had thought that packing her things would make the slightest difference to her situation, she had been a fool. However much she might want to get away from Rose Valley—and at times she did— she was stuck, and she might as well accept the fact. Besides, she certainly couldn't leave now; it was nearly midnight.

The outing into Rose Town had been the first time she had left the ranch. In the few days since Jay's outburst, life had settled into a regular pattern. The mornings were hers, to be spent doing exactly what she liked provided she didn't interfere with Lori's lessons, and that morning, with the prospect of yet another four hours looming emptily ahead, she had gone into the kitchen and, almost unconsciously, had started to help Mike with his work.

She had no idea if Jay knew that she was disobeying his orders, but the patina of polish that she had rubbed into some of the fine old furniture had at least given her the satisfaction of a job well done. It had also, she acknowledged grimly, rubbing until her arm ached, given her the opportunity to work off some of her feelings about its owner on the long neglected wood.

Even so, if Lori had shown some signs of warming to her things might not have been so bad, but Lori was just as hostile and withdrawn as ever, giving the impression that she was continually on her guard.

What was she hoping to achieve? Dulcie had

thought that afternoon when, with Lori beside her, she had been leaning with her elbows on the top rail of the corral fence, watching the men cut out steers ready for market and waiting for Jay to drive them into town.

Her situation was not just hopeless, it was totally unreal—the feeling that she was living on a Western film set as wiry men in cowboy boots and stetson hats roped and loaded the bellowing steers and the almost adult quality of Lori's mistrust.

But what else could she expect? However good her motives for taking the entire blame for her mad dash into the herd, Lori had heard her lie. She knew she had been wrong to do it and she could hardly blame Lori now for not trusting her.

Right and wrong! Black and white! Dulcie smiled wryly at the analogy. Nothing was black and white at Rose Valley Ranch. She was dealing with emotions, and emotions had a way of turning everything all shades of grey, just like the two pairs of eyes on either side of her as she had sat in the dining room earlier that same day, toying with her lunch.

In the way she was beginning to learn that he had of noticing everything, Jay had noticed that she had lost the cream stetson Lloyd had found for her somewhere in the middle of her wild ride through the herd.

'If you don't want sunstroke, you'll need to get another one,' he said, finishing the apple pie Mike had produced for dessert after the inevitable steak. 'I've got to go into town this afternoon. You might as well come along.'

Lori's voice put a stop to Dulcie's unexpected battle between curiosity to see more of the countryside and an irrational but distinct trepidation at the thought of spending hours alone with Jay.

'Can I come too, Dad?' Lori pleaded.

'What about your homework?'

For a second Dulcie thought Jay was going to refuse. So, apparently, did Lori.

'I can do it when we get back,' she offered hastily.

'Okay, fine, then,' Jay relented. 'Ready in the yard in ten minutes!'

'Gee, thanks, Dad!' Lori was already on her feet, all beaming child as she ran out of the room.

Was it possible that Jay had taken something of what she had said to heart and had made up his mind to be less hard on his daughter?

No, Dulcie decided later, it was not. Jay was his usual remote, austere self as he drove the jeep hard and fast along the straight, empty roads.

It was a jeep and not a Mercedes and Jay was in denims and not an expensive city suit, but he was just the same. The disturbing thing was that, in spite of everything that had happened since she had first met him in London, she was more and not less aware of his sheer physical attraction and the effect it could have on her.

It was no use reminding herself of Ross. She had managed to finish her duty letter saying she

had arrived safely, but apart from that, she realised with a jolt of guilty surprise, she had not
thought of Ross for days, and a mental picture of
his dark, good-natured face just could not super-
impose itself over the reality of the straight set
profile with its lionlike mane of hair just inches
away from her.

Because of the emptiness of the country, she
had expected to see Rose Town a long way off,
but the little village took her by surprise. Lost in
so much space, it came up quickly and abruptly
on either side of the dusty road, dominated by the
dazzling bulk of its grain elevators and its one
main street quite quiet and deserted in that dog-
day period of the afternoon before school finished
for the day.

Lori left them the moment they had parked,
diving into the nearest dime store with a promise
to be back, and Dulcie had waited beside Jay,
taking in the unfamiliar surroundings of a feed
store while he transacted the business that had
brought him into town.

'Okay, in here.' He showed her out and then
took her straight into another store, specialising
in saddlery and general Western wear.

'Hi, Jay! Be with you in a minute.' Everyone
knew everyone around here and the store-keeper
only nodded in their direction before he disappeared into a room at the back, leaving them
alone in the fully stocked shop—or store, as
Dulcie supposed she should call it now. Stores,
sidewalks and, when she was talking about a car,

hood and trunk rather than bonnet or boot. That, at least, was what Lori had curtly informed her when they had been looking at the cars and trucks back at the ranch.

So many new meanings; so much, on top of everything else, she still had to absorb.

'I guess this should do.' While she had been considering the strangeness of her surroundings, Jay had been prowling round the store. Now he was behind her, holding a hat similar to the one she had lost. She saw it in his hand—and yet she did not see it. All she could look at when she swung round was the twin reflection of herself in his eyes; two tiny images, head thrown back, lips slightly parted and breath beginning to come shallowly and unevenly as the pulse spot started beating wildly at the base of her throat. However much she might want to deny it, she was looking at the image of a woman who was hopelessly and helplessly on the dangerous edge of love.

It had been the storekeeper's reappearance that had saved her. That and Lori's presence in the jeep on the way home, but there had been nothing to save her from the dangerous self-knowledge that it would be so easy to risk the consequences of a disastrously destructive love affair when she and Jay had been alone together later in the hall-cum-living room of the ranch.

Lori had gone to bed and even the sound of Mike clattering dishes in the kitchen had subsided. Except for the occasional clink as Dulcie put down her coffee cup in its saucer on the now gleaming rosewood table and the sound of Jay prowling restlessly about, they were alone and in complete silence.

She watched him, moving restlessly backwards and forwards across the carpet and the polished wooden floor. He had changed from the denims that he had worn into town, but the expensive sophistication and closely fitting cut of black slacks and a black knit shirt only served to emphasise the feline restiveness of his mood. A prairie lion with a sunbleached mane suddenly finding the confines of a forty-foot room too small for him, and when he swung round on his heel and faced her, his sudden air of purpose made Dulcie say the first thing that came into her head.

'You must let me pay for the hat we bought this afternoon.' Lord, was that really her, sounding so bright and silly?

'Don't be so damned stupid!' Jay's voice told her it was, but he stopped a few blessed feet away from her. 'It's on my charge account,' he said. 'My accountant will settle it when the bill comes in.'

'But I like to pay for my clothes myself!' Once started, she daren't stop. 'I don't want to be under any obligation.'

He studied her with a gleam of derision growing in his eyes. 'In that case,' he said dryly, 'not only are you unique among women but your emancipation will cost you forty dollars!'

'I'll get my bag.' She stood up, relieved to make her escape, but before she could take more than a step or two away, he had completed the move towards her that had made her feel so alarmed and had caught her by the shoulders.

'There are times,' he said thickly, 'when you have no idea how difficult it is not to shake some sense into you!'

The hat that had been the cause of those few seconds of searing self-awareness as Jay's fingers had dug into her shoulders through the thin silk of her dress now lay on her bed, the one thing for which there was no home when she had put away the things that she had packed and then unpacked.

Although she couldn't leave now, when she did go, she would certainly not be taking that hat with her. It could stay here as a reminder of her time at Rose Valley. The only reminder, she had no doubt.

No matter how hard she might try, she could never flatter herself that she had made any real impression. If anything, everything she had said and done had only served to confirm Jay's basic mistrust of women, and although Lori had been slightly less hostile since they had got back from Rose Town that afternoon, the real breakthrough that she had hoped for still showed no sign of taking place.

Who was she kidding? Dulcie mentally lapsed into the vernacular. Although she might no longer show it, Lori still resented her, and the only thing she had achieved by coming to this out-of-the-way part of Saskatchewan was to fall in love with Jay.

No one had ever made her feel like he did; so alive and so acutely aware. And mixed with this was the need to show him that she loved him; to cup his face in her hands and tell him that . . . .

'Stop it!' The words echoed round the empty room, halting a dangerous train of thought that had Jay loving her as much as she could no longer ignore she loved him. She picked up the unoffending stetson and took it to the door. Seeing this reminder of what it felt like to be close to Jay was more than she could bear. She would put it in the hall cupboard; right at the very back!

Lori, dressed in pyjamas and dressing gown, ducked away the moment Dulcie opened her bedroom door, but not fast enough to dispel the impression that she had been hovering there for some time. What on earth for? Dulcie wondered. It could hardly be to eavesdrop. Apart from her own a few seconds earlier, there had not been a raised voice in the house since Jay had abruptly let go of her shoulders and left her speechless in the hall more than two hours before.

'What are you doing, Lori?' she asked.

'I was going for a drink of water!' The reply was also a shade too fast and too defensive to be credible, but Lori was already beginning to walk away when she caught sight of the open suitcases still on the bed. She stopped. 'I didn't mean to, really!' she said in an agonised voice.

'You didn't mean to what?' Dulcie supposed she was talking about being caught outside the door, so what Lori said was totally unexpected.

'I didn't mean to get you killed! That's why you're leaving, isn't it? I suppose you've guessed I made you ride Bowler on purpose, but I didn't want to get you killed—honestly! I just wanted to scare you a bit so that you'd leave—but now I don't want you to!'

The words came out in a jumble that it was hard to understand, but one thing was abundantly clear. Ever since that mad ride into the herd, Lori had been suffering from a guilt that was almost overwhelming and whatever was causing it just had to be sorted out.

'I think you'd better come in.' Dulcie held the door open wider and, with a last desperate glance over her shoulder in the direction of her father's room, Lori walked in. 'Now,' Dulcie asked, shutting the door behind her, 'what were you saying about not meaning to get me killed?'

'You really don't know?' Lori was surprised.

'No, I really don't.'

'But I thought Dad would have told you— about Bowler.'

'He said something, but it didn't make too much sense at the time.' Nothing had made too much sense after that horrific ride. 'Perhaps you'd better tell me,' Dulcie smiled. 'You'll probably feel much better if you do!'

'Well, Bowler's a trick sort of horse.' Lori took a deep breath and began. 'Lloyd just keeps him to try out the men who stop off here for work and shoot their mouths off about how well they can ride. So when you said you hadn't ridden much, I thought it would be kind of neat to put you on old

Bowler. I thought he'd just get tired of you and chuck you off. He does that,' she finished ingenuously.

'And you thought that would be kind of neat!' Dulcie felt her lips begin to twitch, although nothing about the incident had been funny at the time, and she carefully hid her smile. Although it was a relief to know that Lori hadn't intended any real malice, it had obviously cost her a lot to come and confess, and it wouldn't do to let her see that her confession was amusing.

'I guess I was jealous, I suppose,' Lori continued in a barely audible voice. 'Of you and Dad, I mean . . . .' She floundered on. 'There's only been me and him living here before, and when he said that you were coming . . . well, I thought I'd get rid of you. But when I saw what happened and when you didn't tell, I felt like the pits!'

'So you were waiting outside until you could pluck up enough courage to come in and confess?' It all suddenly became crystal clear.

Lori turned her face away. 'I tried last night, but you were asleep.'

'Oh, Laurel!' Feeling genuinely sorry for the child, Dulcie took a step forward.

'Don't call me that!' Lori jerked her head up and faced Dulcie with blazing eyes. 'Just because I didn't want you to think I tried to kill you, it doesn't mean I want to be a girl!'

She swung round and rushed out of the room, dressing gown flying as she disappeared. Dulcie smiled. At least this wild mood swing from apology to anger was better than the cold indifference, to say the best—and downright hostility, to the say the worst—with which Lori had previously treated her. Lori. She must remember to call her that. What was in a name, after all? It wasn't the child's name she had been sent to change.

She had been christened Dorothea Alice after both her grandmothers and she doubted if she had been called Dorothea since her christening. Lori didn't need to be called Laurel to grow up into a woman.

It was the start of a new beginning with Lori, but, as if to counterbalance this improvement, Jay was once more totally austrere and unbending to the point where it sometimes seemed impossible that there could be warm flesh and blood underneath that cool indifference. But, worse than this, as he grew more remote, so he drew Dulcie more—like a star draws a distant satellite—until it became a conscious effort not to fill every waking thought with him.

Peace of mind became a thing of the past. The days when her whole future had been cut and dried with no decision to make other than when she should give up her career and marry Ross now seemed to be part of a tranquil past that belonged to someone else.

She was caught between the horrifying realisation that she was falling in love with a man who at worst despised her and at best endured her presence in his home, and an almost overwhelming guilt about Ross.

Ross had put up surprisingly little argument against her trip. The break would do her good, he had said, studying her anxious face, and besides, he would be coming to Canada at least once while she was there. Now his letters had started to arrive, calm and affectionate just like Ross himself, but even as she read them Dulcie found it difficult to remember him clearly. Another face, with aquiline features under a lion-like mane of hair and eyes that narrowed to regard her with an ever-changing grey as they probed the thoughts behind her words, kept on interposing itself between the words that Ross had written and her mind's eye.

The whole situation was quite hopeless, but she could neither change it nor herself, when a letter from Ross saying that he had definitely arranged a trip to his company's head offices in Calgary kept her awake for hours one night, long after the house had settled into its complete night-time silence.

It might not be a passionate love, but she loved Ross, and she was mad to torture herself with thoughts of love for Jay. She was here on an impulse that he bitterly regretted. He had virtually spelled that out the day she had arrived. He had made love to her in the pool because she had thrown herself at his head and he had rescued her because she had been fool enough to ride a horse she could not handle. What more did she need to tell her what Jay Maitland thought of her!

She slipped a robe over her cotton nightdress. She had to get outside. Her room was stifling after days of hot oppressive weather, building up to a storm that never came, and what breeze there was was defeated by the mesh screens covering the open windows. It must be cooler out of doors, and even if it wasn't, anything would be better than staying here, unable to sleep and unable to stop thinking.

It was dark outside with no moon and the stars a million miles away, and Dulcie stood for a while, letting her eyes adjust to the darkness.

Gradually the colours that the darkness had drained away returned and her ears began to pick up the small night sounds. The swimming pool changed from an oblong patch of black to a sheet of shining silver shot with blue and the prairie lilies on the lawn once more began to hold a hint of their glaring daytime orange in their depths.

The perpetual prairie wind had dropped and, for the first time since she had arrived, everything was completely still, with only the small slap of water against the tiled surround of the pool to keep her footsteps company as she began to walk towards the back of the house.

She passed her bedroom window with the light shining behind the screens and then there was only darkness. It was soothing to walk in the still night and she kept her mind a deliberate blank,

walking aimlessly and without purpose and thinking neither of what had gone before nor of the
problems that undoubtedly lay ahead.

A horse whickered uneasily in a corral somewhere ahead of her and the ground underneath
her feet changed from grass to soft sandy soil. A
few yards further on and a furtive rustling told
her that a small prairie creature had abandoned
the easy foraging near human habitation and
slipped away to find a spot where its solitude
would not be disturbed. Then, once more, everything was still.

When it came, the sound of voices startled her;
raucous and mixed with laughter and the sound
of breaking glass, with Lloyd Southwind's voice
raised angrily above the rest. Jolted out of her
near-trancelike state, Dulcie realised that she had
walked in a wide circle and was now much nearer
the bunkhouse than she cared to be. She could
see the men through the lighted windows and she
automatically turned away. Leaving the confines
of the house to walk up to the one place, above all
others, that was out of bounds was tantamount to
jumping out of the frying pan into the fire.

She could just imagine Jay's reaction if Lloyd
told him he had seen her there.

'Flaunting herself in front of the hired hands!'
might be one scathing comment he would make.
'Causing trouble with the men!' might be another.

Grateful for the noise that had alerted her,
Dulcie walked as quickly and as quietly as she

could back in the general direction of the house. She felt better for her walk. Perhaps if she went to bed now, she could get to sleep.

She saw the shape when she was skirting the first corral. Black like the horses moving uneasily in the background but, unlike them, completely still. At first she thought it was a saddle or some clothes that one of the men had forgotten and left on the rail, but even as she strained her eyes, she knew she was wrong. It was too solid and substantial and then it moved and, quite suddenly and clearly, became the figure of a man looking in her direction.

Her first reaction was that it must be one of the saddle tramps Lloyd had talked about—and she was only wearing her nightdress and a cotton robe—but before she had time to do more than think about changing her direction to escape an encounter with one of these rootless and probably drunken men, the man had called out to her.

'Who's there?'

It was Jay's voice and, for a second, her relief was so great that it almost swamped her usual physical reaction to the sight of him, but he had taken no more than a step or two towards her before her heart began beating in its familiar uneven rhythm and her breath started catching in her throat.

'Who's there? Dulcie? Is that you?' Jay spoke sharply, but as he came closer and saw the pale white oval of her upturned face in the light of the moon that the clouds had just released, his voice changed. 'I'm sorry,' he said gently, 'I must have scared you.'

'That's all right.' Dulcie wished the uneven rhythm of her heart would settle down, but this first apology, combined with this first hint of a personal concern, made it accelerate so wildly that it seemed impossible for him not to hear it. In her ears it was beating like a drum.

'There's no need to be scared,' he said. 'I'm the only person who comes out here at night. Come, I'll walk you back to the house.'

He put out a hand, but something more than fear made Dulcie pull her arm away so that his fingers left no more than a trail of scorching consciousness across her skin.

'There's no need to do that. I mean, I'd like to stay out here a little while,' she extemporised to explain her quick refusal. 'It's so quiet and peaceful,' she added desperately.

'I'm surprised you don't consider that the greater of two evils!' His eyes changed from grey to silver in the moonlight as he gently mocked her.

'The greater of two evils?' Dulcie was genuinely confused.

'Staying where it's quiet and peaceful even though it means staying alone with me.' Was it just a trick of the light, or did his eyes change again as if the casual, half joking interrogation meant more than it implied?

Dulcie shook herself free of the notion. 'We're hardly alone,' she said with an artificial brightness as another burst of shouting mixed with laughter came from the direction of the bunk-house.

'No, we're not, are we?' Jay's face visibly tight-ened. 'How stupid of me to forget! It's only in this direction that there's any illusion of solitude.' He nodded out across the darkness of the corral towards the prairie. 'Otherwise, we've got people all around us. Of course we're not alone.'

He took up the position in which she had first seen him, with his elbows hooked over the top rail of the fence and his chin resting on his hands. It was the sweater casually tied around his shoul-ders that had given him the outline that had puzzled her, she realised.

She also realised that although he might be looking at the horses he wasn't seeing them, and as she studied him from the corner of her eye, the silence began to build a tension and awareness that was almost unbearable.

'How are you getting on with Lori?' His ques-tion came when she thought he had forgotten her and was thinking of slipping quietly away. Sur-prised, she stopped and considered it, forcing herself to pretend a cool professionalism that was scarcely what she felt.

'It's a little soon to say.' The formal note in her voice was reassuring and she clung to it like a drowning man. It helped her to think more ration-ally. Should she tell him about the emotional confession that had marked a real turning point? No, better not, she warned herself. It was safer not to get involved in a discussion about emotions, especially when her own were so close to breaking through.

Jay studied her for a moment and then turned away, either satisfied with her answer or accepting her lack of progress as no more than he had foreseen, and the silence he had broken began to build up again.

'Tell me—you're the expert in psychology— what do you advise if someone is heading towards a situation similar to one in which they've already been badly hurt?' Jay answered his own question before she could reply. 'Ignore it, I guess, and wait for it to go away.'

'Not necessarily!' Dulcie assumed he was still talking about Lori—although Lori was hardly a problem that would go away, even though she was bound to grow up into a woman. 'No two situations are exactly the same, any more than any two people are exactly alike. It could end differently this time.'

'So you'd advise an optimistic caution?' There was an expression on his face that puzzled her. What exactly was he driving at? Dulcie's heart started to beat its old familiar tattoo.

'You could say that,' she answered on a quick intake of breath.

'In that case . . . .' Jay stopped abruptly. 'Have you ever been in love?' he asked instead.

'No.' She answered without thinking and both lied and told the truth. Although everybody had always taken it for granted, she had never been in love with Ross. That was the truth at least; she couldn't doubt it now. Ross had never come near to awakening the agonising depth of feeling the man now facing her aroused. But, by the world's standards, she was in love with Ross. At least, she had never openly disputed the accepted fact that one day they would marry, however much she might have resisted it in her heart.

'You're shivering!' Jay noticed. 'Here, put this on.' He slipped the sweater from his shoulders and held it out.

'It's all right, I'm not cold.' Dulcie backed away.

'Will you stop fighting me and put it on?' He pulled her to him with a rough gentleness. The sweater held his warmth and, with his hands still on her shoulders, she had the sensation of being doubly in his arms. 'Have you any idea,' he asked her softly, 'how difficult you make it for me to apologise?'

'Apologise?' She forgot about her feeling of being in his arms, forgot about everything except her surprise at hearing the one word she knew she couldn't possibly have heard.

'That's right—apologise!' Jay proved her wrong. 'As strange as it obviously seems to you, I *am* capable of regretting some of the things that have happened and of saying that I'd like us to make a fresh start.'

Dulcie could once more see herself reflected in his eyes. Two tiny figures looking incredulously up at him.

'You don't have to treat me any differently

from anyone else, you know!' she said to break the spell.

He laughed, his white teeth glinting in the moonlight and his strong throat curved above her head. 'For God's sake, woman, will you stop trying to be so emancipated or equal or whatever you want to call yourself!' He pulled the sweater more closely together underneath her chin and his laughter died. 'You're shivering again,' he said softly. 'Come on, I'll take you home.'

CHAPTER SIX

THE next morning Jay announced a holiday and, from seeing practically nothing of him, Dulcie was with him practically all the time. Long, hot days riding across the prairie with Lori frisking about on her black pony by their side and Dulcie learning fast on the gentle strawberry mare that Jay had picked out for her.

One day they left the horses and took to the air with Jay flying them as far west as the Alberta border before circling round over the hills to the north and coming back to the ranch in the flat lands of the prairies.

Dulcie had flown in to Winnipeg, in Manitoba, east of Saskatchewan, but Alberta and even Calgary were much closer, she realised.

The one thing they never did was go swimming in the pool. It was strange, Dulcie thought in passing, when she remembered Jay telling her that he always went for a regular lunchtime dip, but even when they were near the house in the middle of the day, a swim was never mentioned. Perhaps Jay went and perhaps he didn't—he had more than once come to the breakfast table with damp and darkened hair—and Dulcie sometimes looked longingly at the clear blue water when she came home hot and dusty from a ride.

But why buck the system? she asked herself. Jay had changed, and that was all that counted.

She had also changed, but it was to the detriment and not the benefit of her peace of mind. She could no longer even pretend that she wasn't in love with Jay, and her love kept on catching her unawares. A look, a certain tone of voice was enough to bring her heart racing to her mouth and then leave her suffering pangs of guilt about Ross.

But what evidence did she have for her wild, secret daydreams that a man like Jay could ever be in love with her? No! Not a man like Jay—she forced herself to be honest—the man, Jay himself. The flesh and bone, emotions and contradictions that had developed throughout a lifetime to become the Jason Maitland III as he was now.

She knew he found her physically attractive— she would be a fool not to acknowledge the surge of physical desire she had aroused when they had been together in the pool—but, apart from that, she had no real reason to suppose he had changed his opinion about women. All women—not just her.

It was just that, for some reason of his own, he had decided that the time had come to end the conflict that had raged between them from the moment she arrived, and that was probably for Lori's sake, not hers.

She had no real need to feel guilty about Ross, any more than she had any need to write to him and try and put some of her doubts and apprehensions about their future into words. When her three months at Rose Valley ended, she would be going back to London and to Ross and everything would be the same as it had always been. The moment she saw Ross it would be different. It was only because she was so far away that she had difficulty in conjuring up a picture of his face against the vivid close reality of Jay's. And it was only at odd moments, such as today, when the prospect of marrying Ross seemed quite impossible.

They had been riding back from a picnic beside the river and, with the scent of home in her nostrils, even her quiet mare had been jogging stubbornly, when Jay had ridden up and laid a hand gently over hers on the reins.

'No, not like that.' He gently unclenched her fingers. 'If you pull at her, she'll pull back, and because she's much more powerful than you are, she'll win. Give her a chance to show that she's a lady! Let the reins go and talk to her!'

He had showed her how and the mare had dropped back into her usual willing walk, but it wasn't until the sight of a single errant calf had taken Jay and Lori riding after it in two separate clouds of dust that Dulcie had been able to rid herself of the frighteningly exquisite sense of feeling that had started in the hand that he had touched and slowly spread to envelop her whole body.

'Gee, this is pretty!' Lori had taken to coming

into Dulcie's room before dinner and now she was standing beside the open wardrobe, fingering the skirt of Dulcie's print silk dress.

A dress! Dulcie could hardly believe it. It wasn't only Jay who had changed. When she had first arrived, Laurel Maitland would have endured torture rather than admit she liked a dress.

'It *is* pretty. Why don't you wear this one tonight?' Lori had taken the dress out of the wardrobe and was twirling round so that the skirt—a delicate haze of pink and green, all colours that should have clashed terribly with Dulcie's red hair but somehow did not—flared out against the background of her blue denim jeans, when her approval was halted by a stupendous crash. The skirt had caught Dulcie's bag, perched on the edge of the dressing table, and the bag was now on the floor with its contents spilling out in an untidy heap.

'I'll get them!' Lori dropped the dress into a second heap and knelt and started collecting the scattered objects.

'Who's this?'

Dulcie was also on her knees, searching for a lipstick that she had seen rolling under the bed, when Lori spoke on a note of guileless innocence.

'Who?' Dulcie turned, enquiring, and then she froze. Lori had Ross's picture in her hand.

'A friend!' Dulcie silently called herself a coward. Ross was more than a friend.

'He looks nice.' Lori turned the colour photograph over. Was there an inscription on the back

or not? Suddenly Dulcie could not remember.
She couldn't remember anything. All she could
think of was that, even if she spent the rest of her
life regretful and alone, she just had to write to
Ross and let him know she couldn't marry him.
It wasn't fair to keep him tied to her. Without
her, he might find someone else.

Ross's letters had slackened off recently, but
that was no excuse for not writing to him, and she
must write before he came to Calgary.

'Are you going to marry him?' Lori switched
Dulcie's attention back to the picture in her hand
with a terrifying accuracy, and Dulcie froze.

Change the subject! Change the subject, she
warned herself. 'He's an engineer,' she said, 'just
like you want to be.'

'Really?' Lori looked from the photograph to
Dulcie. 'Then he's like Mike as well. You know
something,' she added, putting the picture down,
'you ought to ask Dad if you can stay on. We'll
need someone to look after us when Mike's gone
to college.'

It was the look that stayed with Dulcie for the
next few days. A teasing look, challenging her to
accept the casual suggestion, but underneath the
teasing, there was a need that it was beyond a
twelve-year-old to put into words.

She had seen that look before and it puzzled
her until she remembered it had been on Jay's
face that night beside the corral. Surely,
surely . . . . Dulcie brushed the wild hope aside.
She had been mistaken, Lori had her father's

eyes and she had imagined it; any explanation was safer than the wild, heart-stirring hope that Jay could care.

And at least falling hopelessly in love with Jay was not the only thing she had achieved since coming to Rose Valley. Lori had also changed. She was less hostile and aggressive, less completely and utterly resistant to the idea of anything feminine. If she went on as she was, she should certainly have fewer problems when the time came for her to leave her father's private empire and take her place in that half of the world's population that was female.

Lori would always be a continuing sign that she had once been a part of life at Rose Valley, and that, after all, was why she had been sent there, Dulcie told herself. She had not been sent to fall in love with Jay. She had done that entirely by herself.

One afternoon, Lori took her to One Man's Valley, a long ride almost to the western boundary of the ranch where the broad, shallow river that was its lifeblood meandered through a rift cut out by Ice Age glaciers.

It was the only broken stretch of land for miles around, Lori told her, and although even then the prairie didn't rise but dropped sharply into the valley, its slopes were steep and filled with boulders and honeycombed with caves. Some of the caves had never had a man walk inside them, not even the old prospector who had lived there like a hermit years before and given the valley its name.

'You could hide out here for months and no one would find you,' Lori announced knowledgeably, scrambling over the rocks.

'I wouldn't want to, though.' Dulcie shivered. In spite of the bright, hot sunshine, the valley had an eerie atmosphere, full of primaeval ghosts, and its sides were dark and ridged like the hide of a sleeping prehistoric beast. Although man had come late to the prairies, the land itself was old and Dulcie shivered again as she looked around. 'Lori, where's your horse?'

The two active, lively beasts they had brought had been reduced to one. Both ponies were trained to stand without being tethered and Dulcie's strawberry roan was still dozing in the shade of a huge boulder on the valley floor with its reins trailing on the ground, but there was no sign of Lori's frisky black.

'Oh, shoot!' Lori grumbled crossly. 'A gopher or something must have spooked him!' She scrambled down the last few yards of steep, rocky slope and studied the dusty ground beside the hooves of the mildly surprised strawberry mare. 'It looks as if he went off down there.' She straightened and pointed towards a set of tracks heading towards the far end of the valley. 'You hang on here! I'll go and get him!'

'Wouldn't it be quicker if you took ... my horse!' Dulcie's voice trailed away. Lori was already out of earshot, running as if the temperature wasn't in the high eighties and as if the miles they had already ridden, to say nothing of the past hour spent scrambling around the valley, had been no more than a gentle stroll.

'Oh, to be twelve again!' With a sigh of relief, Dulcie sat down in the shade near the strawberry mare and rested her aching back against the boulder.

By the time Lori reappeared, she was worried, really worried. She had no watch, but the land of the midnight sun was only a few hundred miles to the north of them and there, during the weeks of high summer, the sun never set, so that when it began to go down over the rim of One Man's Valley, she knew it was late. Later than they had ever been out alone before. And they still had the long ride home ahead of them when Lori finally reappeared—if she ever reappeared.

Dulcie was walking up and down the valley, telling herself that the next time she turned she really would see Lori coming towards her on the black pony, when she heard a shout. It was Lori —still a tiny figure in the distance, but certainly Lori—but she wasn't riding. She was leading the black pony and it was limping badly.

'I had to go miles before I found him and then he wouldn't let me catch him,' a dispirited Lori explained when Dulcie reached her. 'And I think he must have fallen. Look at his knees!'

The animal was trembling with fear or exhaustion, or a mixture of both, and its head was hanging almost on a level with knees that were bloody and scraped and, even to Dulcie's uneducated eye, already badly swollen.

'I'm not going to be able to ride him,' Lori's voice began to tremble at the hopelessness of it all. 'And, Dulcie, what's Dad going to say?' she wailed.

Dulcie felt like joining her, but it was no use both of them giving up. They just had to get back to the ranch and they had to do it as soon as they possibly could.

'We'll have to take turns,' she said briskly. 'One of us can ride the mare for a bit and the other can walk and lead the pony and then we'll change over. Come on, Lori. You've been doing all the walking—you have first ride.'

The journey home turned into a long, slow, thirsty trek and when the sun eventually went down, leaving a flaring arrow head of purple and crimson across a pale green translucent sky, they still had miles to go. At any other time Dulcie would have thought it beautiful. Now, all she was interested in was how long the afterglow was going to remain before the prairie suddenly became a flat, black table land in which they could easily get lost.

She was the one walking, leading the injured pony, when they stumbled across the private road which led straight to the house. Someone somewhere must be watching over them, she thought with a sigh of relief. It was the one feature of civilisation for miles around, linking the ranch with the main highway into Rose Town, and they could easily have missed it in the dark. She still had no idea how far they had to go, but at least if they kept to it, they could not get lost and it would only be a matter of time before they were home.

She saw the lights of the ranch a long way off and, for a long while, they seemed to come no closer, but suddenly they approached in a great leap and she could see the figure of a man standing in the lighted doorway of the house.

She could also see the plane standing on the landing strip. Jay or Lloyd must have been somewhere that afternoon, she thought tiredly a second before the figure in the doorway spotted them and became Jay himself striding across the lawn.

'Where the hell have you been? I've had men halfway to Alberta looking for you!' Jay's eyes were blazing angrily in the suffused glow of the house lights.

'It's my fault, Dad.' Riding the last lap while Dulcie walked, Lori's voice floated shakily down past Dulcie's shoulder.

'When I want to hear from you, I'll tell you! And get off that horse!' Jay shot his orders in Lori's direction without taking his eyes from Dulcie. 'Have you any idea what time it is?' he asked her. 'Can't you ever be trusted to behave responsibly? Here, take these.' He broke off to take the black pony's reins and give them to Lori.

So much for making a fresh start! Jay was just as hostile and unwilling to listen as he had been when Dulcie first arrived. The last few days hadn't been the real Jay. The here and now was what he was really like.

'Take the horses into the barn and then go and tell Lloyd you're back.' Jay cut across Dulcie's bitter speculations with a curt order to his daughter. 'And get him to take a look at the black, as you seem to have ruined it!'

'But Dad . . . .'

'*Now*, Lori!' His eyes flicked across at her and then back to Dulcie as Lori led the horses off. 'And now,' he questioned her through the sound of muffled hoofbeats, 'perhaps you would be kind enough to tell me where you've been!'

'Does it really matter? They're back now and perhaps we can all get some peace—to say nothing about dinner!'

The voice floating through the open doorway of the house behind them sounded bored. It was also indubitably female. The first female voice Dulcie had heard since coming to the ranch, and evidently belonging to a woman who carried some authority, judging by the way Jay stopped questioning Dulcie and turned towards the house.

'Come inside,' he said abruptly. 'I've got someone I want you to meet.'

He took her arm and brought her face to face with one of the most beautiful women she had ever seen.

Her first thought was that it must be Valerie. Everything about the elegant, dark-haired woman half sitting, half reclining on the chesterfield fitted into the picture she had built up in her mind of Jay's ex-wife. Valerie Maitland, film star! The dark hair combed smoothly back into a severe chignon that would have been unbearably cruel to anyone without the perfect regular features and tiny close-set ears of the woman facing her. And the dark eyes with flyaway corners and long dark lashes gave her perfect face the individual stamp it might otherwise have lacked.

How the camera must love her—and no wonder Jay had married her! Dulcie felt the first, heart-clenching stab of jealousy.

'Dulcie Mortimer—Corinne Patterson,' Jay introduced them.

Corinne didn't move. To anyone standing further away, she would not have seemed in the least concerned and only the faint narrowing of her eyes betrayed her interest.

Corinne Patterson. That must be Valerie's professional name. Dulcie stood there, uncomfortable and on her guard, under the other woman's covert scrutiny.

'How do you do?' She held out a hand which the woman facing her chose to ignore.

'Mrs Patterson's a friend.' Jay sent all Dulcie's preconceived notions about Corinne's identity crashing to the ground, but instead of making the situation better, it made it worse. If she had really been Jay's ex-wife and Lori's mother, Corinne would have had some right to invite herself to Rose Valley to see her daughter. But as a friend, she must have been invited—and invited by Jay, who had spared no pains with her to make his feelings about all women absolutely clear. All women, that was, except Corinne.

But—Dulcie saw a gleam of hope and grabbed it—Jay had introduced her as Mrs Patterson. Perhaps her husband was here, too.

'Darling, how mean of you!' Corinne's mouth puckered into an appealing moue as she glanced up at Jay. 'How can you say we're just friends after all we've meant to each other? After all, you practically saved my sanity when I lost Nelson!'

So much for the missing Mr Patterson. Corinne might have been married once, but she clearly wasn't now; she was a widow, free both legally and psychologically to remarry. There was certainly no grieving in the indulgent look she gave Jay; a look that lingered and caressed before turning into something quite different as her eyes moved on to Dulcie.

That look said that Jay was her personal property and Dulcie would be wise to realise it straight away.

It crossed Dulcie's mind to wonder how Jay liked the idea of being regarded as a woman's personal property, but he was standing behind her and a little to one side and it was impossible to see his face. Not that it mattered. It must have been Jay who had invited Corinne to the ranch; that was all that mattered.

The pink-draped bedroom next to hers, the hat that wasn't Valerie's kept in the hall cupboard for a special guest and, above all, the sudden disappearance of Jay's wedding ring—everything fell into place. What more did she need to tell her that her own wild, foolish love was even more crazy and more hopeless than she had always known it was? Jay was on the verge of marrying for a second time.

'Would you like a drink?' Jay moved away from her shoulder to the glass-fronted cupboard that, since she had begun to help around the house, now held a Waterford decanter and a set of highly polished crystal glasses. Mike no longer had to be called in from the kitchen with whatever mismatched assortment he could lay his hands on.

'Darling, that would be lovely. Perhaps just a teensy one!' Corinne's voice was soft and seductive, but her dark eyes never wavered from Dulcie's green ones. Battle lines had been drawn and she would be wise to know her place.

'I'll get some ice.' Dulcie quickly left the room, but not before she had seen the beginnings of a satisfied smile on Corinne's lovely face.

Dinner was awful, there was no other word to describe it, and it wasn't because they were so late and the meal was dry with heated-up meat and warmed-over vegetables.

Horrified by the amount of One Man's Valley she had brought home with her in the form of dust and dirt streaked liberally over her face, hair, hands and clothes, Dulcie had quickly showered and changed, but the green and pink floral silk dress that Lori had admired so much still seemed as if it had come off the nearest chain store peg by comparison with Corinne's understated and obviously couture elegance.

Corinne, Jay and Lori were already sitting around the table in the dining room when she went in, her hair still damp from the shower and a mass of even more unruly dark orange curls. Corinne wasn't just one of the most beautiful and elegant women she had ever seen, she decided as she took her place. She was *the* most beautiful and elegant, and the most composed and self-assured, with her dark looks a perfect complement to Jay's blond ones. Sun and moon—no, night and day, Dulcie thought as she sat down.

Corinne was talking and she didn't stop. She merely cast a sideways glance in Dulcie's direction with her striking flyaway brown eyes and went on. She was talking about London and she was talking exclusively to Jay.

'I still don't understand why you had to drop everything and come rushing back here. I didn't see any need then and I don't now. Everything looks just the same.' The flyaway eyes glossed over Lori, took in the faded luxury of the lamplit dining room and fastened themselves once more on Jay. Dulcie was invisible. 'I missed the Bensons' party because you left and I had to go to the Covent Garden gala with that idiot Robin Naish!' She went on listing the inconveniences Jay had caused with his sudden decision to leave London.

Underneath her beautiful veneer, she was rich and she was spoiled. Dulcie wondered why Jay was unable to see through her, but he just sat there with his privately amused smile on his face.

The same smile that had been there when he had looked up and said goodnight after driving her to Piccadilly Circus. Dulcie burned. He must have been on his way to meet Corinne when she had stepped off the curb in front of his rented car. It had been embarrassing enough imagining him laughing about the incident—and about her—with an unknown wife. It was ten times worse now that she knew it must have been Corinne.

'Dulcie comes from London.'

It took a second before Dulcie registered her name and looked up to see Jay watching her with a hint of that same private amusement dancing in his eyes.

'Oh, really?' Another pair of eyes, this time dark and anything but amused, glanced reluctantly in her direction. 'Where?'

'Richmond. I shared a flat with two college friends.'

'That's on the outskirts, isn't it?' All of Richmond's riverside walks, its park and its persisting air of Regency elegance were totally dismissed. Corinne re-focussed her attention back on Jay. 'Darling,' she said, 'why don't you come to New York with me next week?'

The conversation went on uninterrupted with Corinne wheedling and persuading. The one person to whom Maitland's law of absolute obedience in his private empire apparently did not apply as Jay seemed on the verge of weakening under her arguments. Lori, at least, thought so.

'I hate her!' Lori's face was reflected in Dulcie's bedroom mirror later that night.

'I hate her, too!' Dulcie would love to have been able to say it. Instead she restricted herself to a mild 'Why?'

'Because she's always coming here and trying to get Dad to go away with her.' Lori picked up Dulcie's hairbrush and tried a few experimental strokes. 'She had a husband once, you know. She brought him here. He was rich but nice—I liked him. No wonder he got rid of her!' she ended on a note of stony satisfaction.

So Corinne was divorced. Dulcie absorbed the piece of information. Why, she wondered, had she given the impression that she was widowed? Perhaps it was to add an appealing air of fragility to her black and white magnolia beauty with its core of wilful steel. But, divorced or widowed, nothing changed the fact that she was still free to marry Jay and, with alimony from a rich husband to live on, she had no need to work. She had made that point more than once during the interminable meal. She had turned down at least one offer to be a model because she preferred to spend her time jet-setting around her friends in Europe and the States.

At least Jay wouldn't have anything to complain about on that score. There would be no career to pull Corinne in two directions if he married her.

'Why are you looking at me like that?'

Dulcie realised she was staring into the mirror, her face hard and set beside Lori's. 'I don't know,' she said evasively. 'I was just thinking.' With an immense effort of will she forced a smile and took the hairbrush from Lori's hand. 'Don't you think you'd better go to bed? It's late and there'll be lessons in the morning.'

But would there? she wondered, when a reluctant Lori had finally left the room. Would Jay want to go back to his old routine or would he decide to take another holiday only, this time, spend every minute in the company of the beautiful Corinne? In New York!

Dulcie mechanically started to undress and get herself ready for bed. She was physically exhausted, but she knew she wouldn't sleep. She began to brush her hair, thinking about Corinne.

Why hadn't Gerry mentioned her? He must have known about her. He had probably known she was in London and it had hardly needed Corinne's pointed remarks during dinner about flying up from the States to Rose Valley whenever she got the chance to prove that she was a long-standing visitor. The pink-draped bedroom was proof enough of that.

Why hadn't Gerry told her about Corinne or considered her a suitable guide to start Lori on the rocky road through adolescence? And, more importantly, why hadn't Jay?

Why had Jay misled her? Why had he given her reason to hope? Dulcie began to brush until her scalp hurt. No! If she was honest, Jay had never given her any reason to hope. All he had done was apologise and say that he wanted them to make a fresh start. That was what she had built her hopes on. To him, she was exactly what she always was—Lori's companion. A woman whom chance and a persuasive friend had thrust into his life for a few months.

Jay had never given her any reason for the fantasies she had started to build in her mind. Fantasies of a life with him and Lori. She had done that herself: basing everything on a few looks and smiles and a few days' happiness.

Dulcie banged her hairbrush back on to the dressing table. If Corinne was asleep next door, *that* should wake her up! So much for the theory that Jay hated women. He might mistrust the sex in general, but, for one member of it, he clearly had no such doubts.

CHAPTER SEVEN

'DULCIE, can you hear me?' Ross's voice waxed and waned with the vagaries of the transatlantic telephone link, but Dulcie could hear him well enough.

'Have you got my letter?'

'Letter? What letter?' Ross sounded surprised and Dulcie relaxed with a sigh of guilty relief. Of course Ross couldn't have got her letter. She had only written yesterday and Ross was thousands of miles away in England.

'Then what's wrong?' she asked with a sudden stab of a different anxiety. 'Why are you calling? It's not because there's something wrong with my parents, or with yours, is it?'

'Wrong? Why should anything have to be wrong for me to call you?' Ross replied. 'And all the parents are fine. No, what I'm calling for is because . . .' he seemed to say something, but she couldn't hear it because of the line . . . 'because I don't know when I shall be getting out to see you. The company's offered me this fantastic opportunity to stop off at their Arctic oilfields on my way across. They'll still fly me down to Calgary in a company plane, but I won't know the exact times and dates.'

'Oh, I see!'

'You don't sound very disappointed,' Ross remarked. 'How are things going, by the way? You've not said much in your letters.'

'Oh, fine!' Dulcie was deliberately vague. 'Look, Ross, this call must be costing you a fortune!'

'What's money?' She could hear him smile. 'But if it bothers you, I won't stay on the line!' Was it her imagination or did Ross sound relieved that she did not want to have a long, intimate conversation? 'I was only calling to tell you that I shan't be able to let you know in advance exactly when you'll be seeing me. I'll have to call you from Calgary when I get there. Oh, and Dulcie, there's something else.' Once more there was the sound of a muffled conversation and this time Dulcie got the impression that he was talking to someone at the other end.

'What have you got to tell me?' she asked when he didn't speak.

'On second thoughts, perhaps it would be better if I waited until I see you,' said Ross. 'It's probably a bit too complicated to explain on the telephone, anyway. But don't worry—and take care!'

They said goodbye and Dulcie replaced the receiver. She was a coward and she knew it. She should have told Ross about her letter and not let him read it by himself when it arrived. But, as Ross himself had said, some things were too complicated to explain on the telephone. Things like telling the man who had expected to marry you almost since he had been a child of seven that you could not be his wife.

Love, she had said in her letter, was the most important thing in anyone's life, but not marriage for marriage's sake.

It had taken the week since Corinne's arrival to get the letter written, a week of agonised doubt and indecision. What reason had she got for telling Ross she couldn't marry him, especially now Corinne had arrived and she knew, more than ever, that her love for Jay was just a dream that could never be fulfilled.

Besides, the moment she saw Ross it would be different. The moment she got back to England, one look at his familiar face as he swept her up into his arms would dispel all doubt and everything would be as it had always been between them.

But it wouldn't; she knew that. Deep down, whether she had never met Jay or not, she had always known that she and Ross were not right for each other as man and wife. Loving friends, yes, but not partners in a lifelong contract, and if she married him, it would be to fulfil her parents' expectations, not her own. Ross did not deserve a marriage in which she would always be looking for something—or someone—else.

So she had finally written her letter, one of the hardest things she had ever had to do in her life, and had given it to Lloyd to post in the main post office in Calgary, just an hour or so's flight away, before she could be tempted to change her mind.

A curious sense of freedom had washed over her as she had stood and watched the plane take off, but she wasn't free. She had known it then and she knew it now directly she heard his voice.

'Bad news from home?'

Dulcie spun round from the telephone.

Jay had come in unnoticed and her sudden movement brought her up against him, brushing the muscle under the knitted green silk shirt and so aware of her need for him that she could have wept.

Why, oh, why had he had to come in now when, for a whole week, she had avoided ever being alone with him? Why had he had to choose just this moment, when her defences were so low that it would have been so easy to sway just that fraction of an inch more and find herself in his arms?

Instead she stiffened and tilted her head to look him in the eye. 'Bad news? No,' she said defensively. 'Why should you think that?'

'Because you looked so forlorn and dejected standing here all by yourself by the telephone—that's why I guessed the call was from England.' He studied her with a little smile. 'Your parents must miss you to call from England.'

'Yes, I suppose they do.' There was no need to tell him it had not been her parents on the line.

'And you must miss them?' he said.

'Not particularly.' Unable to bear his closeness any longer, Dulcie deliberately moved away. 'I haven't lived at home since I started university.'

'Of course, how stupid of me!' He was no

longer gentle and concerned but cynical and bitterly amused. 'I'd forgotten you were an emancipated career woman with an all-demanding and satisfying career to make family ties redundant!'

'That's an unfair thing to say!' His cynicism touched her on the raw.

'Is it?' He waited for her to disagree again and, when she stayed silent, went on in the same mocking tone of voice, 'It certainly makes what I was going to ask you even more pointless than I already thought it was.'

'What were you going to ask?'

'I was going to suggest that you stayed on when your three months is up.'

To free him to go to New York with Corinne, no doubt! Dulcie angrily beat down a sudden flare of hope. Corinne must have persuaded him to make the trip. She had been harping on nothing else since she had arrived, and with Corinne, the usual laws of Maitland's empire did not apply. While he would not tolerate argument from anyone else, Corinne could wheedle and smile and pout and simper—all done like a spoiled child and all done for effect—and Jay just sat there with a quietly indulgent expression on his face.

'I'm afraid staying on is quite impossible,' she said stiffly. 'I promised Gerry I'd be back at the clinic in another month.'

'And we mustn't let anything interfere with that, must we?' he said caustically. 'No, don't go!' He stopped her as she turned towards the sanctuary of her room.

'I have to change for dinner.' She looked down at her denim skirt, half consciously, also, looking for a place to hide. But there was nowhere. She and Jay were quite alone in the empty hall without even the sound of Mike clattering dishes in the kitchen to offer her protection.

'That can wait.' She heard Jay coming closer and struggled to control the uneven breathing that would have given her away. 'I want to know why you're avoiding me.'

'Avoiding you? I'm not avoiding you.'

'So it's my imagination, is it, that every time I come into a room, you can't wait to leave?'

'That's hardly true,' she countered. 'We're in the same room every mealtime.'

'That's not what I mean and you know it!' He gripped her by the shoulders, forcing her to look up into his set face, so that she could once more see twin images of herself reflected in the steel grey of his eyes. This time, however, there was no moonlight and he was not wrapping a soft cashmere sweater round her shoulders and talking about making a fresh start, he was challenging her to deny his allegation, and she turned the challenge back.

'What you mean, I suppose,' she said with a cool control that surprised her, 'is that you don't feel able to keep up a civilised mealtime conversation with me.'

His hands tightened on her shoulders with a bruising pressure. 'Have you any idea how difficult it is to get through to you sometimes!' he asked her thickly.

'How silly of me! I thought I heard the bell for dinner!' Corinne was standing in the doorway watching them and although butter might not have melted in her mouth, one look at the expression on her face would have frozen it.

'In that case you were wrong!' Jay abruptly moved away. 'We don't have bells round here. Mike always shouts, remember.'

No wonder he sounded angry. To say the least, he had been found in a compromising situation with his daughter's companion. Dulcie wondered where they had been. She had vaguely heard the sound of the aeroplane landing when she had been on the telephone to Ross and Corinne was wearing a beautifully tailored pale linen suit with a flash of colour in her hand which was a silk scarf for her, as always, immaculate hair. And Jay was in grey slacks with his green knit shirt, rather than his more usual denims, and there was a pig-skin jacket on the chair just inside the door as if he had dropped it there when he had come in.

Perhaps they had flown to Calgary—the oil capital of Canada and exactly the sort of boom town to buy a replacement for the wedding ring Jay no longer wore and another, more elaborate one, for a woman like Corinne.

'Excuse me.' Dulcie finished the escape she had begun minutes before. 'I have to go and change.'

It was hopeless, absolutely hopeless. She was putting herself through purgatory, and to what end? Instead of changing for dinner, she should be packing her things and calling Ross and telling him there was no need for him to come to Canada because she was coming home.

But she went on mechanically changing from the clothes she had worn all day into the long patterned paisley skirt and cream silk blouse that complemented her mop of red curls so well and set off the honey glow that, for the first time in her life, her skin had begun to acquire—yet another irony of the almost film set unreality of her life.

The hours spent out in the open air with Lori, riding or leaning with her elbows on the top rail of the corral fence watching wiry men in cowboy boots and hats rope and load the bellowing steers, had achieved what the annual ritual of her holiday with Ross had never done. Spain or the South of France left her looking like a boiled beetroot unless she took care, but here, in the clear air of Saskatchewan, she looked her best.

She could tell it from the sideways looks the hired men shot in her direction a few mornings later when she was standing beside the corral watching them cut steers ready for market out of the milling herd that had been driven into the pens. Looks that made Lloyd Southwind shout angrily as a steer escaped a carelessly thrown lassoo and thundered back into the protection of its fellows.

It fascinated her to watch the horses and the way they seemed to understand what was required of them almost without command. A man on horseback was still the most effective unit for cutting out individual animals, Jay had once told her. You could use a jeep, a truck or even a helicopter for rounding up the whole herd, but when it came to breaking down the mass into smaller groups and then into individuals, the traditional way of one man, one horse, working as a team, was still the most effective and the most economical method.

So the Old West was re-enacted for her enjoyment every time market day came around, and with or without Lori, she found herself irresistibly drawn to the dust and noise and sheer primitive excitement of the corrals.

But now she unhooked her elbows from the rail. She was wanted here no more than she was wanted anywhere at Rose Valley. Lori still needed her, but soon that need would be past and she would have absolutely no excuse for staying on once her three months was up. No excuse at all, except her own hopeless, self-destructive need to be near Jay on any terms.

Hearing another angry shout from Lloyd, she began to walk away. Jay and Lori would still be in the schoolroom—the morning routine of lessons went on in spite of Corinne's arrival—and a sulky Corinne had driven off in the Porsche that morning, so there would be no one in the house to see her dejected entrance. Dulcie Mortimer, career girl, aged twenty-five, who had always known where her future lay—before Jimmy Bruce, that was, and before Jay.

'Hi, beautiful!' A man detached himself from the shadow of the barn and stood blocking her way.

'Excuse me!' Deciding to ignore him, Dulcie stepped to one side.

He sidestepped to stop her in an odour of stale liquor mixed with sweat and smiling what was meant to be an ingratiating smile with a mouthful of dirty teeth. 'Hey, not so fast! You've been giving me the come-on all morning—you're not going to switch off now!'

'The come-on?' She had never seen him before in her life.

'Sure!' The smile broadened. 'Back there at the corral. I saw you watching me'— he spat—'so did that damned Indian!'

Light began to dawn. This must be one of the men she had been admiring when she had been watching them round-up the stock. Impressive on horseback and of a piece with his horse as he had checked and galloped and skilfully lassooed the plunging steers, but far less impressive now with his leering eyes and the thoughts that were obviously running through his head.

'I'm sorry.' She tried to retrieve the situation without a scene. 'I wasn't watching you in particular. I was just watching what was going on.'

'Aw, come off it! I've got eyes in my head, ain't I? There's no need to git shy. Tell you what,' his manner changed to become confidential, 'why don't you take off to town with me? I've just about had enough of this stinking place, anyway.

Why not come with me and have a drink and see what happens from there?' He smiled again, flabby with beer, but still much too strong for her to be able to push her way past.

'No, thank you.' Dulcie began to get alarmed. She couldn't run and they were quite cut off at this corner of the barn, and if she couldn't see the house, no one in the house could see her. He had chosen his spot well, and if she was going to get past him it would have to be on wit alone. 'I have to go in for lunch,' she said calmly. 'Mr Maitland's expecting me.'

Jay's name had some effect. At least, some of the man's confidence began to drain away, but not enough to stop him catching her arm as she went by and pulling her close to him. 'I'll just give you something on account, then, to show you what you're missing in case you change your mind!'

'You've got fifteen minutes to get out before I break your neck!' Neither of them had heard the footsteps coming round the corner of the barn, and now Jay's voice cut through the odour of stale sweat and beer and the fingers that gripped her arm released her as if scorched. The man looked up past Dulcie's shoulder.

'I wasn't doing nuthin', Mr Maitland! Just a bit of fun!'

'Fifteen minutes!' The force of Jay's anger filled the space between them and the man who had posed such a threat now seemed insignificant.

'What about me things?' he whined in a last effort at belligerence.

'Get them!'

'And me wages?'

'Get them from Lloyd!'

'Yes, sir ... no offence meant, ma'am!' He edged carefully past Jay and disappeared around the corner of the barn; a paper cowboy in work-stained clothes.

'Thank you!' If Dulcie had expected sympathy or concern, she had been wrong. When she turned and looked up at Jay, he was looking at something, or someone, over her head.

'Don't thank me,' he said offhandedly. 'It was pure chance that I was out here at all. I was worried about Corinne.' He nodded, and a persistent noise that Dulcie had been vaguely conscious of for some time became the engine noise of the Porsche, approaching at speed along the dirt road leading to the ranch and trailing a cloud of dust. 'Incidentally,' Jay's eyes flicked down, expressionless behind long lashes, 'now that you've had first-hand experience of the reason why, stay away from the hired hands. You may think you can deal with anything, but there are some situations even you can't control!'

He strode off towards the barn just as Corinne brought the Porsche to a screaming, slewing halt inches away from the closed double doors. Dulcie could see her laughing up at him as he approached, her whole face alive with the excitement of driving a powerful car at breakneck speed on the edge of safety. Spoiled, wilful Corinne, to Dulcie—but the perfect complement to Jay.

'She's going to get him to marry her, isn't she?' Lori put the thought that had been in the back of Dulcie's mind all day into words. 'If she does,' she threatened, 'I'll run away!'

'And miss finding out what it's like to have a mother?' Dulcie stopped rubbing her hair and looked at the sullen little face reflected in her dressing table mirror.

'She'll never be my mother!' Lori retorted fiercely.

'She *could* be your friend.' Dulcie doubted it, though, and when Lori had grudgingly left after the ritual of their early evening conversation, she began to wonder what would happen to Lori if Jay married Corinne. No, *when* Jay married Corinne. She must get used to the idea as an almost accomplished fact. All the signs were there. His indulgence, his concern for Corinne's safety out alone in the powerful car—there were so many pointers and they all contrasted with his almost indifference to her own brush with her would-be seducer. In fact, as he had made it so clear that he regarded the incident as far more her fault than the man's, she was surprised that he had even bothered to send the man away. But then perhaps hired help was just as easy to come by as it was to lose. She had noticed a battered pick-up truck making its way to the bunkhouse during the afternoon and it had still been parked there later.

Presumably a replacement had been hired already.

She finished drying her hair and began to dress. She would be leaving Rose Valley in a few weeks anyway and could bury herself in her work until some of the emotional scars had begun to heal, but Lori's whole world was at the ranch. What *would* happen to her? Dulcie was dejected and depressed when she left her room and walked along the corridor to the hall for another ritual that had been introduced since Corinne's arrival: pre-dinner cocktails.

'Ah, Miss Mortimer!' A shadow moved and became Corinne, sitting on the chesterfield in the hall, her grey silk dress blending almost perfectly with the mottled light streaming in through the open doorway. 'I'd been hoping for a word with you.'

Unlike the shadows, Corinne's perfect face was hard; hard and clear-cut like the diamonds sparkling in her ears.

'Really?' Dulcie was suddenly on her guard. Corinne was predatory, waiting to spring. She wondered if Jay ever saw that side of her.

'Yes, really, Miss Mortimer!' Corinne mimicked. 'I wanted to ask what you think you're doing here.'

'In this room?' Dulcie was puzzled.

'No! Here—at the ranch!' Corinne's voice was sharp with exasperation, but the question was so unexpected, it took Dulcie off her guard.

'But surely Jay explained,' she said, surprised.

'I'm here because of Lori.'

'Are you?' Corinne's beautifully plucked eyebrows rose in sceptical half moons. 'Are you really here because of that brat—or are you here because of Jay?'

'I don't know what you mean.' Dulcie began to turn away, but Corinne stopped her.

'Oh, come now, you're not as stupid as all that! Jay did give me some cock-and-bull story about having you here to straighten Lori out, but isn't the truth more along the lines of you meeting him in London and then persuading that well-meaning idiot Gerry Herrendeen to send you out here so that you could follow him? I don't think we have to say what for!' Corinne ended pointedly.

'That's a totally uncalled-for thing to say!' Dulcie felt her colour rising to match her anger. 'Besides which, it's not true!'

'Isn't it?' Perhaps Corinne caught the fractional unsteadiness in Dulcie's voice and her eyes narrowed as she readied to attack. 'Then why are you always mooning round him with those big green eyes and baby curls? Has he taken you to bed yet?' she asked maliciously. 'Because if he has, I hope that's all you want—because that's all you're going to get. Jay's not the marrying kind— or at least, he thinks he isn't. One day, perhaps, I'll let him persuade me to change his mind, but not now—not until he's got rid of that brat of his to university or wherever she wants to go!'

In her last few words, Corinne was honest— totally honest about her feelings for Lori—and Dulcie shivered.

'But in the meantime,' Corinne went on more smoothly, more like her usual drawling self, 'we suit each other. I take care of his needs and he takes care of mine——' Her eyes flicked over Dulcie's face. 'I'm sure I don't have to explain,' she said derisively. 'No one can be that naïve in this day and age, not even you, I think, Miss Mortimer. Jay and I see each other whenever we choose and for the rest of the time we're free to lead our own lives, whether it's in New York, London, Paris or here, in this godforsaken spot!' She glanced around with distaste.

'It sounds a very satisfactory arrangement,' Dulcie got out through stiff lips.

'It is, I do assure you.' Corinne gave a feline little stretch. 'But it's an arrangement for two people, not three, and that's where you come in— or rather, *don't*! It strikes me the time has come for you to leave.'

'That's not a decision I can make,' Dulcie flashed back, refusing to be cowed. She might know that she was feeling sick and humiliated, but she was determined Corinne shouldn't see. 'I committed myself to stay here for three months and there's still some of that time left.'

'In that case, it's a decision Jay will have to make, isn't it?' Corinne said equably. 'I'll have a word with him—tonight—when we're alone. I shan't put it like that, of course, and it would be ludicrous to imagine Jay would even see it in that way, but what it really boils down to, I suppose,' she gave a little laugh, 'is that he's going to have to make a choice between the two of us. You see, my dear Miss Mortimer, although you may be prepared to share a man to get him, I am not. It's you or me, and although I very much doubt that Jay will even see it as a contest, a choice is what he's got to make.'

'It would seem then that I'm being presented with an ultimatum for the second time in my life!'

Neither of them had noticed him come in, but Jay was standing there, in the entrance to the corridor leading to his room, and for once, even Corinne was abashed.

She got quickly to her feet. 'Darling, I didn't hear you!' She went up and took his arm and snuggled close to him, making a halfhearted effort to turn the whole thing into a joke. 'You know how women are—half the things they gossip about, they're not even taking seriously themselves!'

'Don't belittle what you said, Corinne.' Jay's reply was completely unexpected. 'It made me realise that a decision I've been trying to avoid has got to be made—and made tonight.'

'But, Jay . . . .' Corinne began again, anxious and alarmed; no longer the spoiled little girl.

Jay interrupted. 'I made a decision once, and it cost Lori her mother and me my wife. I have to talk to you, Corinne, and I should have done it days ago.'

Was Dulcie the only one to see Lori standing in the passage behind her father with a look of stricken comprehension on her face as Corinne's alarm gave way to an expression of quiet triumph? Not that it mattered, Dulcie told herself, dinner was strained and tense enough as it was, with only Corinne chattering brightly with that same look of elation sparkling in her dark eyes.

And Corinne had cause to be elated. Dulcie compared her glitter and brilliance with the dull insignificance of her own misery. Corinne had got what she wanted: she had Jay and she herself had fallen out of the frying pan into the fire. She had been sent to Rose Valley as an antidote to the guilt and depression that had overwhelmed her after Jimmy Bruce's death, and now she was in the same house with the man she loved while he was asking another woman to be his wife.

Dulcie had no doubt that was why Jay had asked—almost ordered—Corinne to take coffee with him in the schoolroom after dinner. And neither, she was sure, had Lori, sitting on the other side of the board and playing a game of Scrabble on which neither of them could concentrate. She looked at the tightly shut-up little face: the hostile, defiant child who had greeted her arrival was back again. But how could she comfort Lori when her own heart was being torn apart? And how could she have been stupid enough even to hope that Jay could ever have been in the slightest way attracted to her—when he already had Corinne?

She remembered the hardness of his body in the swimming pool and the punishing brutality of his mouth. She had been wrong in thinking that it had been anger that had driven him. It had been hunger, not anger: and a hunger that had once more been satisfied since Corinne's arrival at the ranch. Even without Corinne's obvious hints, Jay's aura of powerful masculinity was such a part of him that he was hardly likely to go through life a monk.

But what, she wondered, long after the game of Scrabble had been abandoned and she and Lori had gone to bed, what did he and Corinne have to talk about at such length?

'Will you marry me?' The words were simple and quick enough to say and Corinne's one word of acceptance even quicker. But they were still closeted in the schoolroom.

Perhaps they were discussing a marriage settlement. Both divorced, they had some cause to mix romance with prudence. Jay was rich, even though life was lived so simply at Rose Valley, and Corinne was clearly also wealthy. Her clothes, her jewels, her travels around the world—if they were talking about a marriage settlement, they would have a lot to talk about.

But perhaps it was Lori's future they were planning. Even Jay would be blind not to realise that, although she might be more than willing to be his wife, Corinne was certainly not anxious to take on the role of Lori's mother. The memory of the expression on Corinne's face when she had been talking about Lori was still enough to make Dulcie shiver.

So maybe it was boarding schools and not marriage settlements Jay and Corinne were discussing. Boarding schools, and the early departure of an English girl along with Lori which would leave them free to be alone to start their married life.

How could Jay marry someone like Corinne? Why couldn't he see through her? Caught up in a fury of anger and frustration, Dulcie began to work off her feelings on her pillow, aware as she did so of another noise behind the dull thumping of her clenched fists. She stopped and listened. It was the Cessna, revving up to take off.

She went cold. Surely . . . surely Jay hadn't allowed Corinne to persuade him to leave without a word to Lori? But then none of Jay's normal rules seemed to apply when it came to Corinne.

Picking up her cotton robe and throwing it on over her nightgown as she went, Dulcie raced to Lori's room. If she could hear the plane, then so could Lori. And if she could guess that Jay was leaving with Corinne, then Lori could as well.

She flung open the door, but the room was empty with the bed not slept in, just creased and crumpled as if Lori had been lying on the coverlet for some time, also without sleeping, before deciding to get up again.

Where was she? Dulcie glanced round desperately. The one thing she could be sure of was that Corinne would never have allowed Jay to take Lori with them. She looked down at her bare feet. There was no time to go back to her room for slippers. She just had to get out to the plane and try and stop Jay before he took off.

At first the grass was cool and smooth under her bare feet, but then she had left the lawn and was wincing and stumbling over sandy, stony soil as she ran wildly in the direction of the airstrip, calling and shouting, even though she knew she was too late as a brilliant spotlight scythed the darkness and the plane took off.

Dazzled and half blinded, she caught sight of a figure in the afterglow. It must be Lloyd. Still half dazzled, she ran on towards him.

'Lloyd! You've got to help me! Lori's gone!'

'Gone? Gone where?' The voice was much closer than she had expected, and it didn't belong to Jay's Indian foreman, it belonged to Jay himself. A second later, breathless and still only half comprehending, she was in his arms.

'Where's Lori gone?' He pulled her closely to him as she stumbled, scanning her face with quick, anxious eyes.

'I don't know!' she managed to gasp out. 'But she must have heard the plane and thought you were leaving with Corinne!'

'She thought what?' He sounded totally shocked.

'That you were leaving with Corinne to marry her!' Dulcie began to waver. What had seemed so obvious only a few minutes earlier now seemed much less certain. 'Isn't that what you plan to do?' she managed to ask.

In answer, he cupped her face in both his

hands. 'What on earth put that idea into your head?'

'You did!' With every second now telling her that she was wrong, she went on quickly above the still audible noise of the departing plane. 'I thought—we both thought—that when you said you had a decision to make, it must be to marry Corinne. I think that's why Lori's run away.'

Jay's thumbs dug into her jawline. 'Because she thought I was going to get married or because she thought it was going to be Corinne?' he asked her urgently.

'Corinne, I think.'

The pressure on her jawline relaxed and, even in the dim light, she could see the quick relief that softened the normally harsh lines of his face. 'In that case,' he smiled confidently, 'I don't think we should have any problem in getting my runaway daughter to come back should we? Not when she knows that it's you I plan to marry—not Corinne!'

CHAPTER EIGHT

'You haven't given me your answer.'

Stunned and still only half believing, Dulcie stood in the hall and watched Jay's eyes turn from light to shining, darkest grey.

Lori was in bed and asleep. Jay had found her in one of the barns, too scared to follow her original intention of leaving on her motorcycle in the dark, and he had carried her back to the house, confused and slightly tearful, but apparently content that Corinne had gone. Now she was in bed, already half asleep, when Dulcie had closed the bedroom door, and Dulcie was still in the robe and nightgown in which she had run out to try and stop the plane, feeling the full force of Jay's eyes as he waited for her answer.

Why couldn't she say yes? The impossible had happened. The man she loved had asked her to marry him. It was what she had always wanted—or it seemed like always, even though it had been only a few short weeks.

'Is it Lori that's stopping you?' He came up and read her hesitation.

'No!' She was heartfelt in her denial.

'Your job? Corinne, then?' He went on before she had a chance to explain that her job was the last thing she had thought of. 'Let me tell you

about Corinne—once,' he said vehemently, 'and
then she's part of a past that has nothing to do
with us. There was an affair—years ago, soon
after Valerie left me.' Dulcie noticed how difficult it still was for him to mention his ex-wife's
name. 'I was just divorced and Corinne's marriage was breaking down. It was nothing important and it was soon over—at least, I thought it
was,' he added quietly. 'Obviously I was wrong.
Corinne got into the habit of coming here and
sometimes I'd see her when I was abroad—I
should have stopped it then.' He spread his
hands, more vulnerable than she had ever seen
him. 'But now it's over—you've got to believe
that. You've also got to believe how much I want
you!'

He went to take her in his arms, but Dulcie
drew away. A shadow of the past still stood between them. Was it Valerie or was it Ross?

'It's too sudden—too soon.' She tried desperately to find a reason for her hesitation.

'It's neither sudden nor soon,' Jay contradicted. 'I've known I wanted you ever since a
stubborn redheaded girl rushed out in front of
my car and I found that although it was easy
enough to drop her off at Piccadilly Circus, it was
much more difficult to get her out of my head. I
wanted to, I promise you that!' A hint of the old
Jay appeared in his resistance. 'But you were
there—under my skin—a part of me. That's why
I was as scared as hell when you arrived.'

'You were scared?' Remembering his almost

overwhelming hostility, she forgot everything else. 'You were more hostile than anyone I'd ever met!'

'I was scared,' he corrected her with the beginnings of a smile. 'And what do you do when you've scared the hell out of yourself?—you fight back! I was terrified. I'd thrown aside principles I'd sworn I'd never break until I died. No involvement—casual affairs, that was all. I was never, ever going to allow a woman to get under my skin again. I played that game once and lost. Retired hurt, I think the expression is.' His lips twisted in a mocking line. 'But there you were and I had to face it. It had cost me a swimming pool for that darned clinic of yours to get Gerry to agree to try and persuade you to come out here, and all I could think of when I saw you getting out of the plane was how to make you turn tail and leave!'

'*You* asked Gerry to persuade me to come here?'

'What else are friends for?' He gave her a lazy grin that made her heart turn over. 'I daresay he wouldn't have done it if you hadn't needed the break, and I'm darned sure he wouldn't have done it if he'd known how long that break was going to last!' He cupped her face and his last words were almost lost. 'I need you, darling, and I want you—more than I've ever wanted anything in my life.'

He pulled her to him, hungry and yet tender, kissing her face, her hair, her half-closed, fluttering eyes.

So this was what it was like to have him need her, something she had dreamed of but never thought would happen. She released her breath in a long, husky sigh. If he didn't stop, she was going to let him make love to her. She had no more control over her own reaction than she had over the daily rising of the sun, and she felt hollow and quite weightless when Jay lifted her and carried her down the corridor past her bedroom to his own.

His bed, covered in a spread of soft dark fur, was wide and apparently limitless. At first he was a moving shadow, glinting bronze in the strange half light coming through the window, but then he was beside her, heat searing through the thin cotton of her negligé as he untied the ribbons at her neck so that his mouth could follow the course of his fingers as he brushed the robe aside and slipped her nightdress from her breasts and shoulders.

'Jay!' Instead of struggling, she moaned his name, arching her body and pulling him even closer with fingers tangled in his mane of hair.

'Jay!' Her voice again. No, not her voice! A man's voice, harsh and rough and mixed with the sound of urgent knocking. Jay raised his head.

'What is it?' he asked brusquely.

'It's fire, boss, fire!' It was Mike and he was at the door.

With a swift gesture demanding silence, Jay got up and pulled on a dressing gown, leaving Dulcie with such a sense of complete bereavement that at first she found it difficult to comprehend the hurried conversation going on at the door.

'What do you mean, fire?' Jay was blocking Mike's view into the room with his broad shoulders, but Mike was obviously too alarmed to notice anything.

'It's a grass fire!' he said quickly. 'Coming down over the ridge. Boss, you gotta come!'

Jay turned his head towards the window and, as he did so, Dulcie realised that what she had taken to be moonlight was a disturbed and flickering glow.

'He's right, Jay.' Lloyd Southwind's voice joined the conversation at the doorway. 'It's running along the ridge towards the north-west section and it's running fast! I flew over it on the way back from Calgary.'

'Get the men! Tell them I'm coming, but get them all out and get the tractors. We've got to plough a firebreak round the ranch!'

Dulcie was already re-tying the ribbons at her neck when Jay closed the door and came towards her; no longer the lover but hard and purposeful.

'Get Lori and get her dressed,' he ordered. 'Then wait for me here. Whatever happens, don't either of you leave the house until I get back.'

Fire! The constant threat to the dry lands of the prairies and the forests to the north, destroying millions of acres of timber and grazing land every year in a part of the country where the annual rainfall was considerably less than in any other agricultural area in Canada. A flash of lightning, a carelessly thrown match—anything could start it, and start it so easily that it spread with frightening rapidity with a noise like an express train, consuming everything in its path and changing direction with the wind or its own internal vagaries—but stopping it was often beyond the power of man, even with all man's modern technology. Nature had control of fire and man could only battle and hope she would relent.

Too fascinated to be frightened, Dulcie and Lori watched from the window of Lori's room. Hosepipes ran across the stretch of lawn between the house and the trees, run out without regard to the damage to the grass in the cause of a greater urgency and turning the luxury of a swimming pool into a utilitarian reservoir essential for the protection of the ranch.

The sound of water was deafening, like a heavy tropical storm, as men hosed down the house and barns to keep them damp. They were invisible at first, identifiable only by shouts and shouted warnings, but then the fire crested the ridge and turned them into demonic figures outlined against the glare as it poured down into the swale.

At the last second it checked, turned by the firebreak that had been ploughed and going on less certainly towards the greater firebreak of the road, sensing defeat and flickering and dying around the edges as the men turned their hoses on it and others came up to beat it with sacks.

The fire spared everything except the bunkhouse. Just when it seemed all over, a shower of sparks, blown by the wind, ignited in the smouldering ashes and a tongue of flame leaped across the strip of beaten earth protecting the house and buildings. One of the pine trees went up like a pitch-soaked torch and more sparks showered, this time on to the cedar shingled roof of the dry old building, and it burned like tinder with no hope of saving it.

Had she dreamed what had happened? Her nostrils full of the acrid smell of wet ashes, Dulcie stood in the yard the following morning and wondered. She had not dreamed the fire—the evidence was in her nose and in front of her eyes as she looked at the blackened and charred remains of the old bunkhouse—but the Jay who had made love to her had disappeared.

She glanced at the man standing at her side. He was withdrawn and silent with lines of weariness turning his face into a strained mask with no sign of the luminous tenderness of the man who had asked her to marry him.

Things said in passion were often not repeated the next day. Dulcie racked her brains to account for the change in him. He'd slept on it—he'd had second thoughts. Except that he had not slept at all; he had been out all night dealing with the fire. And as for passion—Corinne's departure and Lori's disappearance had created not a passion but a hunger, a need for sexual release from the emotions of the day, which he had used the word marriage to satisfy.

It might have been love that had destroyed her defences, but for Jay it had been pure need, and she shuddered at the consequences if Mike had not come knocking at the bedroom door exactly when he had.

No—Dulcie beat down her physical response to the memory of those few minutes—Jay had chosen to forget that anything had taken place and she would be wise to do the same.

'Right, get the men and pull the rest of it down!' Jay nodded towards the bunkhouse and, jolted out of her introspection, Dulcie was appalled.

'Sure, boss!' Lloyd, however, on the other side of Jay, seemed to understand. He walked away with a look of quiet approval lighting his dark eyes.

'But why?' The house was a ruin, but it could still be saved. The charred brick walls, housing the charred iron bedsteads from the men's dormitory and a kitchen stove standing drunkenly on one side, were still standing and the steep shingled roof and intricately carved wooden verandah could be replaced. It had been a fine old house and Jay had the resources to restore it. Dulcie felt a pang of real regret at the disappearance of this reminder from another age.

'Why?' Jay looked at her sombrely. 'Because it was full of memories, and not happy ones at that.' He looked back at the building, seeing it as it was. 'Two failed marriages—my parents' and then mine—and a childhood in which the Indian kids out on the reservation seemed better off than I was, even though I was the "rich whitey's son". I thought marrying Valerie might change things——' he stopped abruptly and then went on. 'I haven't set foot in it since the day she left. It was pretty enough,' he agreed quietly, 'but it's best it's gone. And now,' he turned on her and on a startled Lori who was coming towards them with a sudden change of mood, 'to show you just how full of remorse I am, we're leaving Lloyd and the insurance people to take care of this and the three of us are going to Calgary.'

Lori stared. 'But why, Dad?'

'We're going to celebrate the end of the past,' he switched his eyes to Dulcie with a fleeting reminder of the night before, 'and the beginning of the future.'

They flew west, with the sun, to Alberta. At first over miles and miles of sunbaked prairie which gradually became dotted with small oil pumping stations, endlessly bobbing on their cantilevered mechanisms like giant drinking birds as they raised Alberta's black gold up from the Jurassic layers to the network of pipes just below the surface of the earth.

Dulcie could see the pattern of these pipes as they flew on, marked by the changing play of light and shadow in the fields. She could also see, constantly, out of the corner of her eye, the profile of the man who had made love to her.

But it was only her response that proved that it had happened; Jay's face told her nothing. Half hidden in wraparound sun-reflecting glasses and set with concentration as he piloted the plane, it could have been the face of a handsome stranger.

Apart from that one fleeting, perceptive glance when they had stood looking at the burned-out bunkhouse there had been no reminder of the night before and, rather than blaming herself or Jay for what had happened, she should be thankful. Knowing his basic opinion of all women, what might he be thinking of her now if the hot, passionate minutes had been allowed to continue uninterrupted? That she was an 'easy lay', perhaps?

'I can see the mountains!' Lori's voice came from behind her shoulder and Dulcie took her eyes from the plane's controls and from the strong, sure hands that had brought her to a fever pitch of awareness as they had slipped her robe and nightgown to her waist. She looked ahead.

There, in a vast natural bowl, was Calgary and there, like a gleaming, sugar-frosted rim on the edge of a champagne glass, were the Rocky Mountains. Jay banked the plane, pivoting it around the tall central spire of Calgary's communications tower like a ball running around the edge of a roulette wheel, before the earth tilted back to become level and they started their descent.

'I'll taxi her into the hangar for you, Mr Maitland.' A man in spotless white overalls with the name of a private flying club emblazoned on his breast pocket got out of a brilliant yellow tender the moment the plane came to a halt and opened the pilot's door. Another man, in equally spotless overalls, came around the other side and helped Dulcie and Lori down.

'Fine, Stu.' Jay, long-legged and powerful in the closely fitting levis and cotton shirt that did nothing to detract from his intrinsic air of authority, accepted the offer without further comment. 'I'll probably be wanting her again Thursday.'

'Any time, Mr Maitland. Just give us a call and we'll have her gassed up and ready. Oh, and the limo that you ordered's over there.'

He nodded towards a black Cadillac into which the second flying club employee and a uniformed chauffeur were already loading their luggage. With life lived so simply at the ranch, it had been easy to forget the wealth that backed it up and the well oiled efficiency that only money and the influence it brings can buy, but, sitting in the Cadillac, separated from the chauffeur by a glass partition, Dulcie felt almost overwhelmed by a degree of luxury that she had never known before.

'Impressed?' Jay was watching her as the car slid silently out of the airport and turned away from town.

'Yes, but——' she frowned as the thought struck her. 'Where are we going now?'

'To Aunt Julie's, of course.' Lori supplied the answer. 'Didn't Dad tell you?'

'You mean to say Jay didn't say a word?' A

hint of Jay's amusement struggled for mastery over incredulity in Julie Lancaster's face. About thirty, Julie also had her brother's mane of dark blonde hair and the assured tilt of his head and neck, fined down on her more slender shoulders, but the lines that could give Jay's face such a stern, forbidding look were, in Julie, softened so that instead of power and authority she radiated a verve and vitality that made her immediately approachable.

Dulcie liked her. She particularly liked the way she laughed, wrinkling a smaller version of Jay's nose.

'Oh, well,' she said, 'I suppose I shouldn't be surprised. Getting any sort of personal information out of Jay has always been rather like mining for nuggets of gold! He didn't tell me about you, either, and judging by the change in him since he was here last, I should say that's far more significant!' She shot Dulcie an amused, sidelong look. 'My big brother——' she rolled her eyes. 'Come on, I'll show you to your room.'

They went up a boad, softly carpeted staircase which branched when it reached the level of the crystal chandelier so that two short flights continued up to the landing running all around the upper level of the hall. Julie turned right and led Dulcie down a passage carpeted in the same dove grey and opened a door into a bedroom that looked out over the back of the house.

The big Georgian-style mansion was part of an exclusive housing estate some miles out of Calgary and the only sounds to be heard were the voices of Lori and the horde of Lancaster children playing in the garden beneath the half open window.

Jay and Dick Lancaster, Julie's oil executive husband, were somewhere in the house below, and, as Dulcie took in the luxuriously furnished room and the panoramic view of Calgary in the distance, she became aware that Julie was studying her.

'Do you like it?' Julie was obviously referring to the room and Dulcie nodded. 'Good,' Julie went on calmly, 'then you and Jay can have it when you come and stay with us after you're married. Jay can make do with Dick's dressing room this time.'

As well as looking like him, Julie also had her brother's knack of taking your breath away.

'Married? We're not going to get married!' Dulcie managed to get out.

'Aren't you?' A small dimple appeared at either side of Julie's generous mouth. 'Then you must be the one who's going to be doing the refusing, because Jay's got all the signs of asking you. Don't forget, I know my brother, and I was still living at home when he married Valerie. He had something of the same look he's got now about him then. Not that it lasted long, of course. Things soon started to go wrong.'

'Julie, what did go wrong? What was Valerie like?' Dulcie fingered a small silver stud box on the dressing table. She had to know and there was something about Julie Lancaster that made the questions easier to ask than they might otherwise have been, but the answers still frightened her.

'Hasn't he said anything about that, either?' Julie's eyes darkened, studying her in the mirror.

'No.'

'He should do,' Julie said flatly. 'The catharsis would do him good. He needs to talk all his feelings out and see what his marriage really was—a mistake from the very beginning without a cat's chance in hell of ever being a success.'

'I'll tell her, Julie!' Dulcie spun round. Jay was standing in the open doorway, his footsteps noiseless on the thick carpet. Dulcie couldn't read the expression on his face, but Julie obviously could, and she walked across and kissed him on the cheek.

'I'll make sure you're not disturbed,' she said. 'But remember, big brother, if either of you need me, I'll be downstairs.'

With a last reassuring smile at both of them, she left the room, closing the door quietly and turning the few yards of dove grey carpet separating them into an impassable gulf.

Jay's stillness frightened Dulcie. The responsibility was too great to take. A million and one reasons for not wanting to hear what he had to say flashed through her mind. 'You don't have to tell me anything,' she said.

'No, Julie's right.' All sense of panic and isolation vanished as he came up and laid his hands gently on her shoulders so that he could look down into her face. 'It takes more than a fire and the destruction of a houseful of memories to make a new beginning. It takes trust and honesty—things that have been sadly lacking until you came into my life. I should have been honest with myself about Valerie years ago— before we were even married.'

'*Before* you were married?'

He smiled at her surprise. 'That's right. I was crazy about her, but deep down, I knew we weren't right for each other and, to do Val justice, she never pretended that we were. She never made any secret of the fact that for her, her career came first, last and always. I doubt she would ever have said yes if I hadn't asked her on the night she heard that her first big film break had come through. She was in a mood to say yes to anything that night, and I persisted—God knows why I did!'

His face grew sombre and he went to stand beside the window, his hands in his pockets, looking without seeing at the garden.

'I persisted because I wanted to break the Maitland jinx,' he continued. 'To prove that even though my parents and grandparents had both had unhappy marriages, I could be different. I should have left that to Julie, I guess,' he added as the sound of children's voices floated in from the garden. 'Julie and Dick were made for each other, just as I kept on telling myself that Valerie and I were. She was the most beautiful thing I'd ever seen.' He paused. 'Dark-haired, slim, with the sort of skin that looked as if it would bruise if you so much as touched it. But her skin was the only fragile thing about Valerie!' Dulcie could hear his whole face tighten. 'Otherwise, she was tough and totally dedicated to her career. She left me the moment she found out she was pregnant . . . babies and a career didn't mix, she said.'

'But what about Lori?' Dulcie asked.

'Lori was born in Hollywood,' Jay said shortly. 'I went down to get her and I haven't seen Val from that day to this. Money and lawyers freed me from my marriage, but I was left to do the rest myself. I had to get rid of my own bitterness, and I found I couldn't do it. Julie's right.' He turned unexpectedly back from the window, his mane of hair blazing in the sun. 'I should have talked about it, got professional advice, but instead I nursed it and let it grow until it wasn't just Val I was bitter about. It was all women, even my own daughter!'

'And now?' Dulcie found the courage to probe him gently.

'And now?' He came back to her and put his hands lightly but possessively on her waist and looked down into her eyes. 'Now that shadow's gone and I want an answer to the question I asked you last night. Darling, I love you. Will you be my wife?'

CHAPTER NINE

'SOMEWHERE in my youth or childhood, I must have done something good!'

The song had always been a favourite, and the words went through Dulcie's head every time Jay took her in his arms for brief, snatched seconds whenever they could be alone.

His kisses held a passionate gentleness that perhaps not even he had known he had possessed and the overbearing, hostile Jay of her arrival had disappeared, leaving him younger and so much more vulnerable that sometimes Dulcie felt not only the wiser but the older of the two.

The ring was a two-carat diamond solitaire, to be set on a narrow gold band that would complement the later wedding ring, but it was still in design form when they left the premises of the Calgary diamond merchant from whom Jay had arranged to buy it. Swamped by the discreet luxury of their surroundings, Dulcie had sat speechless as tray after tray of stones were brought for their inspection and she could still hardly believe that the diamond she had last seen glittering on a piece of black velvet would, when she next saw it, be on her finger as her engagement ring.

Jay's face reflected in the glass partition of the

limousine as they drove away. He smiled at her and a lump caught in her throat. It was too much happiness; almost too much to hold and, like a fragile crystal, it could so easily be shattered.

Lori's had been the first voice to break the silence when Jay had announced their engagement at the Lancasters' the night before.

'But what shall I call you, Mom or Dulcie?' Lori had asked.

'What do you want to call me?' Dulcie enquired.

Lori looked thoughtful. 'Dulcie, I think. Well, at first, I guess. We'll see how things turn out,' she added in an old-fashioned way, but then another thought struck her and she beamed. 'Can I be a bridesmaid?'

'You'll have to wear a dress,' her father warned.

'Oh, gee, Dad, will I?'

Lori's crestfallen expression had provoked a gale of laughter, but even as she had laughed with the rest, Dulcie had suddenly thought of Ross and a small cloud had seemed to pass across the clear summer sky outside the Lancasters' drawing room window.

Having taken shape and form, the cloud remained, and as the days went past, it grew. But why should the thought of Ross disturb her? Why should she be frightened of telling Jay about a childhood romance that had developed only because of the pressure of other people's expectations? She had written to Ross and she was free.

Ross would not be coming to Calgary now. All she had to do was explain to Jay, just as she would have explained immediately after her breathless acceptance of his proposal if he hadn't then driven everything from her mind with a kiss that had destroyed all capacity for thought.

But, rather than calm her fears, her rationalisation only made them grow more daunting. She had to do it. What was stopping her? Without this last confession, where was the truth and honesty that Jay had talked about?

Calgary helped. Rich and expanding fast, there were times when she could almost hear it growing.

Home of the Calgary Stampede and once the centre of Alberta's grain and cattle industry, it had been taken over by oil, and the huge steel and glass towers of the international banks and multinational oil corporations were marching out to overtake and dwarf everything, even the stockyards and the Stampede grounds themselves.

Dulcie had been born and brought up in the shadow of London, one of the world's largest cities, and for two years she had lived and worked right in the centre of it all, and yet, in just a few weeks at Rose Valley, she had become so used to the peace and isolation that Calgary was almost overwhelming, and she found herself gawking at the sights like any country tourist.

The outward signs of the oil boom were everywhere. In the smartly dressed women thronging the stores with their couture clothes and expensive jewellery and in the young executives marching briskly through the network of glassed-in walkways and upper level shopping malls that made it unnecessary ever to set foot outside their air-conditioned comfort to shop or browse.

Once she saw Ross and her stomach clenched, but then he turned and became one of the young oil company executives, a little like Ross but much more like the rest.

'What's wrong?' Jay noticed her sudden hesitation.

'Nothing.' Dulcie made herself smile up at him. Nothing's wrong, she went on silently, except that I have to tell you something and I'm so frightened of losing you.

If only she had someone she could talk to. Her parents? No. She had already persuaded Jay to delay calling them, frightened that they might mention Ross. Perhaps she could talk to Julie. She glanced at Jay's sister out of the corner of her eye. Surely with her wide and generous mouth and laughing eyes, Julie would understand the dilemma that had crept up and overtaken her. A dilemma that grew worse as every day went past, making it more difficult to break her silence and compounding her deceit.

They were in the powder room of the luxurious Four Seasons hotel, softly lit except for the theatrical lighting around the make-up mirror, and discreetly scented. Jay had brought them all out for dinner on their last night and he and Dick Lancaster were waiting in the dining room, talk-

ing over the fine brandy Jay had ordered to
round off the meal.

'Gee, we'll have to go—the baby-sitter!' Julie
had caught sight of the sunburst clock reflected
in the mirror. 'I promised her we'd be back by
twelve and I've got to drive the kids to swimming
lessons first thing in the morning.' She grinned,
smoothing down the flurry of pleats over her
slender hips. 'Now you know what keeps you
slim after having five children! Running round
after them! Not, I daresay,' she added with a
glance in Dulcie's direction, 'that you'll need to
worry about putting on weight when your brood
comes along! You know,' her whole face changed
and became serious, 'Dick and I are so delighted
that we're going to have you as a sister-in-law.
We wanted you to know that.'

'Thank you!' Dulcie found it hard to meet her
eyes.

'You're what Jay's needed for years. It's a
shame you weren't around before he met Valerie—but I guess you were still in knee socks
then,' Julie added with a trace of her brother's
teasing in her smile, taking in the softly plunging
olive green silk dress that, resisting Jay's efforts
to buy it for her, Dulcie had splurged on in one of
Calgary's most expensive boutiques earlier in the
day. 'And as for that Corinne . . . !' Julie made a
face. 'Just think, all those years I spent worrying
about that brother of mine when it was all a complete waste of time!' She laughed at Dulcie's
expression of surprise. 'Fate was bringing you

two closer all the time,' she explained happily. 'And it's not hard to see how crazy he is about you. I hope you've not got a thing against children, because I suspect you're going to have some, and I insist on being godmother to my first nephew!'

She went on and on, making it more impossible for Dulcie to unburden herself about Ross with every word, and then the chance was gone. Dick was driving them back to the big house overlooking the lights of Calgary and then Dick had gone again, taking a sleepy-looking baby-sitter home and Julie, Dulcie and Jay were standing in the hall.

'Coffee, you two?' Julie took off her wrap and headed towards the immaculate chrome and glass kitchen.

'Mm, sure, that would be nice.' Jay didn't even wait for Julie to disappear before he took Dulcie in his arms and was kissing her with a passionate hunger that made it impossible for her to think. All she could do was feel—feel the thin covering of soft green silk melting away as he pulled her against the hardness of his body and feel the heat of his lips as he brushed the softly curling tendrils of hair aside and buried his face against the scented pulse spot leaping wildly at the base of her throat.

'Dulcie!'

Jay didn't even pull away when Julie's voice, sharp and disbelieving, came from the direction of the kitchen.

'Dulcie, there's a message for you.' Julie came up to them with a sheet of paper in her hand and Jay released her slowly and reluctantly, keeping one arm around her waist and holding her close to his side. 'Mindy must have forgotten when we came in—the baby-sitter,' Julie explained. 'She'd pinned it up on the bulletin board in the kitchen. It's from a Ross Sutherland. He called. I couldn't help reading it. He said he's your fiancé and that he's in Calgary.'

Dulcie was still cold minutes later. Cold from the sudden icy rigidity of Jay's body and cold from the look of scathing contempt that had filled his eyes. He had released her instantly, as if the touch of her offended him, and had walked from the hall into the living room without a word.

'Julie, I can explain!' Dulcie's voice shook and she raised her hands in a helpless little gesture.

'I don't think I'm the one who needs the explanation.' Like her brother's, it seemed impossible that Julie's eyes could have ever held any warmth. 'I think you should go and talk to Jay.'

He was standing in the living room with his back to her when she went in, and the room which had once seemed so warm and friendly with its apricot curtains and scatter of softly shaded table lamps beside each piece of furniture was full of the brooding anger showing in the rigid lines of Jay's shoulders and the muscular tension of his legs.

'Jay, I can explain!' She could have reached out and touched him, but the gulf between them was suddenly impassable and when he turned, the bitterness in his eyes was so intense that, instead of taking a step forward, she moved back.

'I'm sure you can,' he said with a thin-lipped smile. 'You've no doubt had an explanation ready for days in case just such a situation as this arose. What is it?' he asked viciously. 'What were you going to say? Something along the lines of "I'm sorry, Jay, but this thing I've got going with Ross is bigger than both of us?" Or,' his face changed as he finished his stinging parody of the old movie dialogue, 'was I going to be the lucky fellow? Now that you've seen all this——' the sweep of his hand took in all the discreet opulence of the house, '—had you decided that I was the better bet and that Ross Whoever-he-is could have saved himself the trouble of coming chasing after you!'

'That's unjust!' A quick flare of anger mixed with the tears that she was struggling to hold back.

'Yes, I think it is.' For a second she had a glimpse of the man who loved her. 'I don't think even you'd do that,' he finished quietly.

Dulcie took advantage of his change of mood. 'Ross is a childhood sweetheart. I've known him for as far back as I can remember. Our parents have always hoped that we'd get married, and perhaps, at one time——' she paused; this was the difficult part of what she had to say, the part she should have confessed to days before. 'Perhaps, at one time, I thought we'd get married, too. But

now now—not for a long time now. Jay, you've
got to believe me!' She offered up her face for his
inspection, praying he could see the truth of what
she said.

'Have you any idea how much I want to believe
you?' he said in the same low voice. 'It's not pleasant to believe that I've made the same mistake
twice in my life, but there's too much of what you
say that doesn't make sense—and too much that
does!' he finished savagely. 'Why, for instance,
does he leave a message saying he's your fiancé
and why, if you mean so little to each other,
should he come all this way after you?'

Why had Ross come to Calgary? Dulcie didn't
know. He must have got her letter and now the
last thing she had anticipated had happened.
How easy it would have been to have told Jay
about Ross compared to this. She might have lost
him then; she had definitely lost him now.

He stood there, waiting for her answer.

'Ross is in the oil business,' she began. 'He's a
chemical engineer.'

He broke into her explanation with a laugh that
made the sinews in his neck stand out like cords
above the incongruous formality of his dinner
jacket and bow tie.

'That's good,' he said rawly. 'For a story made
up on the spur of the moment, it's very good.
The only problem is that it's just a little too perfect. It's too much of a coincidence that this non-
fiancé of yours would be in the one business that
would bring him here. Try not to insult my intel-

ligence.' He came close, almost touching her. 'Why, Dulcie, why?' His eyes bored into her. 'And don't tell me it was love,' he warned her sharply. 'That's the one thing you've never told me. Do you realise that? You've never said you loved me. Why not, I wonder? A last truce of that famous honesty?'

He waited for her to answer, but she couldn't. He was right—not in the way that he supposed, but he was right. The thought of Ross had always been hovering over her like a shadow.

Jay misread her agonised silence. 'So,' he said, 'we've reached the truth at last. What was I—a challenge? A last affair before you settled into the joys of wedded bliss?' He turned the words into an insult. 'But maybe that's wrong too. I'd forgotten that you're an emancipated woman! And if you can have a career after you're married, why shouldn't you have affairs, too? A few scalps to hang from your emancipated belt! You've always been ready enough to give yourself to me, as I remember. . . .' His eyes glittered dangerously, reminding her of those few humiliating moments in the pool the day after she arrived. 'Let's see if I can make you want me again, shall we?'

He pulled her to him, crushing her mouth with his, and even while she was sobbing and struggling in his embrace, tasting the salt of tears on her lips and wincing under the ruthless pressure of his fingers as he clamped her wrists behind her back and used his free hand to wrench her dress down from her shoulders, Dulcie knew that she was weakening. Even though her mind cried out that it was lust, not love, and revenge, not tenderness, that was driving him, she could not stop her whole self moving closer with her need for him, and there was no pride, just deep overwhelming longing, in the hoarse cry that escaped her.

'Jay! That's enough!' Julie's voice, calm and incisive, came from the door, backed by the sound of a car pulling up in the driveway outside. 'Dick's back—whatever you two have to settle can be settled in the morning.'

Dulcie read Ross's message when she got to her room, holding the sheet of paper in fingers that still trembled slightly. Ross, her fiancé, had called. The baby-sitter had written the message in a neat schoolgirl hand; a message that had brought two people's happiness crashing to the ground. Her fiancé was in Calgary and he would call her again tomorrow.

She re-read the words that had done what she had not had the courage to do for days; tell Jay about Ross. And now it was too late. She still couldn't marry Ross, but she had lost Jay. She knew it as surely as she had seen the look of pain mixed with contempt that he had given her as he had walked out of the softly lit living room past Julie and on up the stairs without another word.

One word in the message caught her eye again. Her fiancé—she crumpled the paper into a ball in a spasm of misery. Why had Ross called himself that? It never had been true! And why, oh, why hadn't she told Jay?

She flung herself face down on the bed. Somehow she had to get through this night and the following day. Somehow—no matter how much it cost.

The hardest part was putting on a show in front of Lori. Sitting at breakfast in the dining room, Dulcie wondered if Lori noticed that Jay never quite looked at her. He spoke to her as little as he could—and Julie barely spoke at all—and when he did, although his voice gave no hint of the emotion that surely must be racking him, his eyes stayed hard and grey, fixed on a point somehere above her head.

'But why isn't Dulcie coming back with us?' Lori asked for the umpteenth time, pushing the remains of her breakfast around her plate with her fork. 'Is she coming back tomorrow?'

Jay avoided the direct question. 'She's staying in Calgary because she has someone visiting—from England.' His voice barely wavered. 'Don't you think you ought to go and find Aunt Julie and thank her for having us? The car will be coming to take us to the airport in a minute.'

'But, Dad ... !' Lori's voice rose to a grievance.

'*Now*, Lori! I'll have Lloyd fly out and get you if you want to come back to the ranch and get your things.' Jay turned to Dulcie as the sound of Lori's dragging footsteps died away. 'Otherwise I'll have them crated up and sent after you.'

'But what about Lori?'

'What about her?' Jay was deliberately callous. 'She'll survive. We both will. In time, perhaps we'll both come to regard the whole episode as an interesting lesson—let's hope that your fiancé will be more fortunate and that he'll get what he thinks he's getting—an honest, loving wife!' The telephone began to ring. 'Or is that too much to expect of any woman?' he finished savagely.

'Jay, you must let me explain!' Dulcie heard footsteps going across the hall and the ringing stopped. 'Ross and I have never been engaged!' She held out her ringless hand in a futile effort to convince him, but before she could gather her thoughts to go on, Julie was standing in the doorway, her unsmiling face such a contrast to the sun-filled dining room.

Her voice matched her face. 'Dulcie, you're wanted on the telephone. It's your fiancé.'

Dulcie had two overriding memories to keep her company in the taxi taking her to downtown Calgary: the stranglehold of Lori's thin arms wrapped around her neck to say goodbye and Jay getting into the limousine that was to take them to the airport without a backward glance. And that had been her last sight of him. It had been Lori's face that had been glued to the rear window as the car went down the drive and, unless she could ever summon up the courage to go back to Rose Valley Ranch, all her hopes and dreams had disappeared as the car turned out of the driveway.

Now there was Ross to face. Ross in the downtown hotel he had chosen for their meeting. One more person to hurt and disappoint before she could be free to pick up the shattered remnants of her life. All in all, she had quite a tally. Lori still not knowing that the bridesmaid's dress she had packed so carefully in her suitcase was never going to be worn. Julie, tightlipped and scarcely speaking out of loyalty to her brother and Jay . . . . Dulcie's heart clenched in a quick spasm and she forced her mind away.

About the only person she wasn't going to disappoint was Gerry. There was no doubt now that she'd be going back to her job at the clinic at the end of her three months' leave of absence. Her career—the only thing she had left and, for the first time in her life, it meant absolutely nothing.

'You don't look as well as I'd expected!'

Although lipstick disguised the faint puffiness of her lips and a tailored linen suit made sure that the marks Jay had left on her shoulder when he had wrenched her dress away the night before were safely hidden, the shadows underneath her eyes and her tired, drawn expression were past disguising and Ross noticed them.

'What's wrong?' he went on, half joking, half concerned. 'Doesn't the land of the blue-eyed oil sheikhs agree with you? Or is it that wild and woolly cattle baron of yours who's causing your problems?'

'He isn't mine, and his name's Jay Maitland,' Dulcie responded stiffly.

'I'm sorry!' Ross gave her a sharp, discerning glance. 'I was only teasing. I didn't come here to quarrel. Taking what I said like that isn't like you.'

Dulcie looked at him; at the concern that filled his eyes and the stocky reassurance of his familiar figure. He was so nice! Why, oh, why couldn't she have fallen in love with Ross? Why did it have to be Jay who had turned her normally ordered life upside down and made every other man a second best?

'I'm sorry, too,' she said with a flash of quick contrition. 'And I'm sorry about what I had to say in my letter.'

'Letter? What letter?' Ross was surprised.

'The one I wrote about two weeks ago.'

'Then it must be waiting for me back home.' Ross smiled, satisfied. 'I've been up north at the company's oil sands plant in Athabasca for the last week. Your letter must have arrived a day or so after I left. What did you say in it?'

Dulcie took a breath. If part of her destroyed peace of mind was not telling Ross face to face that she could not marry him, her chance had come. 'I said,' she began slowly, 'that I didn't think we were . . . .'

'Your coffee, ma'am.' A waitress leaned across and put the cup in front of her, and by the time she had served Ross and left, Ross had taken charge of the conversation, suddenly diffident and ill at ease.

'Dulce, I've got something I must tell you.' He fiddled with his coffee spoon, his hesitation and his use of the old, familiar nickname taking her back about ten years to when a gangling Ross had asked her for their first grown-up date. 'I should have written, I suppose, but somehow the right words just wouldn't come. Not that I didn't try,' he added vehemently, 'often!'

'Ross, there's something wrong, isn't there?' She remembered his hesitation on the telephone when he had called the ranch and her voice was sharp.

'In a way.' He looked up, meeting her eye for the first time. 'Except that it's not so much what's wrong. In fact,' he took a breath, 'I'm here because I had to tell you that you were right.'

'Right?' She was thoroughly confused.

'Yes. Do you remember the night when you were deciding whether to come to Canada or not? You said something about us having been conditioned into getting married because that's what everyone expected—rather as if we'd had no say in it ourselves?'

'Yes, I remember.' She recalled the conversation well. Still in the depths of her depression about Jimmy Bruce, her defences had been down and she had talked more openly about her doubts about their marriage than she had ever done before.

'Well, you were right,' Ross said almost aggressively. 'Not that I thought so at the time and I missed you like hell when you first left, but then I started to talk to one of the girls at work about you. It was just to talk about you at first, but then, quite suddenly, we weren't talking about you any more, we were talking about us. I don't know how it happened, Dulce,' he said earnestly, willing her to believe him, 'but I'd fallen hopelessly in love. I know it sounds ridiculous, but it seemed to happen overnight.'

Oh, no, it didn't sound ridiculous! She, too, had fallen in love in what seemed the space of one second to the next and her life would never be the same again. Looking at his familiar face, crumpled in his efforts to explain without hurting her, Dulcie suddenly felt closer to Ross than she had in all the eighteen years they had known each other.

'It's all right,' she whispered. 'I understand.'

'I knew you would—or rather, I hoped you would.' Ross's face cleared with relief. 'She's a wonderful girl,' he went on confidently. 'You'll like her. Her name's Rovera.'

'What?' Dulcie couldn't help exclaiming.

'Yes, I know, it's ghastly, isn't it?' Ross grinned for the first time. 'It's half her father's name and half her mother's: Ron and Vera. I keep telling Kit that they probably wanted a dog and not a daughter. You know—Rover,' he explained as she looked puzzled. 'Anyway, I call her Kit. She's small and blonde with blue eyes—oh, and you'd like her, Dulcie, I know you would.' He was once more seeking her approval.

'I'm sure I shall!' His quick relief brought a sense of utter desolation. 'When are you going to get married, or shouldn't I ask?' she forced herself to say.

'Well, we hadn't actually made any plans. I thought as I was coming over here anyway, I'd tell you first—and Kit agreed with that,' he added hastily. 'But now, you know, I don't see why we shouldn't go ahead and make plans for some time next month. We both want a quiet wedding, and there's no point in waiting when you're both as sure as we are. It's funny, isn't it? All those years of you and me together, and now . . . .' Ross's voice tailed away.

All those years and now Ross had been the one to find and keep the rightness that Dulcie had always known was missing and she was left with a career—and an empty space where her heart should have been. A sudden thought struck her.

'Ross,' she said intensely, 'when you get home, destroy my letter. It doesn't matter now!'

'If you say so.' Ross was still too relieved to be curious. 'But aren't you coming back quite soon yourself? I was hoping you'd be at the wedding.'

'I don't know.' Dulcie avoided a direct answer. 'I might be staying on a while.'

Her explanation must have satisfied him, because her last sight of Ross was of him smiling and waving as she drove away in the taxi from the hotel. But what was she going to do now? she thought dully as the taxi stopped for the pedestrian crosswalk in the shadow of the Calgary Tower. She had told Ross that she was going back to the Lancasters' and had let him assume that she was then flying back to the ranch with Jay and Lori.

What she had most certainly not told him was that Jay and Lori had already left earlier that morning and that she was facing a future that was so empty that even her emotional reaction to Jay's rejection could not penetrate the void.

She sat there watching the stream of brightly dressed people filing to and from the Calgary Tower. Most of them were probably on holiday, planning to spend some time on the observation floor at the top of the Tower with its view of the city and the Rocky Mountains.

Dulcie had been there once with Jay and Lori and the two elder Lancaster children and she could imagine the excitement and anticipation of the people streaming past, yet she stayed remote, uninterested, as if she did not have the slightest human connection with them.

She could only think of Jay. Jay with his arm around her shoulders as they had stood and looked at the view of the city far beneath them and at the mountains circling the horizon. She could also see Jay in those mountains, at home at last in her imagination with his muscularly economical way of moving as they had walked for hours around the sapphire unexpectedness of Lake Louise, not talking but just savouring the unexpected bonus of a whole day alone together.

Jay—she could only think of Jay. It had seemed incredible then that he had loved her, and it now seemed almost inevitable that he did not. She felt numb and curiously disorientated for the next two days, as if the effort of telling the taxi

driver to take her to a randomly chosen hotel and
then booking herself in had drained her of the
capacity to make any more decisions.

She supposed she would go home. She had
money—Jay had left a cheque with Julie which
Julie had insisted that she take—and she had her
return·air ticket to England. She also had the
anonymous air-conditioned womb of the hotel
room in which to lick her wounds and stay until
she was sure that Ross had left Calgary and that
she would neither meet him on the streets nor see
him on the flight home.

How ironic it was that it was Ross, who had
never done her any harm in her life, who had
brought all this about. No, it wasn't Ross. She
had done it to herself. If only she had told Jay;
but if only Ross had not left a message as her
fiancé.

'I couldn't seem to get through to the girl who
answered the phone at all,' Ross had explained
when she had asked him why. 'She sounded half
asleep, so I thought it might wake her up a bit if I
told her I was your fiancé. You don't mind, do
you?'

No, Dulcie had said, she didn't mind. Ross
couldn't have known and the baby-sitter couldn't
have known. The baby-sitter! She couldn't even
remember her name and she would never see her
again in her life, and yet ... for the want of a
nail, a horseshoe was lost and for the want of a
horseshoe, a kingdom was lost.

The old rhyme about disastrous events stemming from small beginnings kept running through Dulcie's head when she woke on the third morning of her stay in the hotel. She stared at the reflection of her twisted curls and pale, lacklustre face. It was only her eyes that, for the first time since she had come into that room and hung the Do Not Disturb notice on the door, held any hint of her old self in their depths.

What was she doing? She shook her head and the heavy grey cloud inside it began to disperse. Whatever had happened, she loved Jay. She always would. Was she really going to let him go as easily as this? And Jay loved her—at least, he had for a while. She went and pulled back the curtains and got into the shower, refusing to let the thought of his face, twisted with mockery and contempt, deter her.

She had always fought for what she wanted. Her parents had been against her going to university, saying there was no need as she was going to marry Ross, but she had persisted and she had gone.

That had been the right decision, and so was this. She was going back to Rose Valley to tell Jay that she loved him. She would let fate decide what happened next.

CHAPTER TEN

THE ranch was deserted when Dulcie finally pulled up in the rented car at the end of the private road. Perhaps the hired hands had been let go because of the fire—there was certainly no sign of anyone near the old barn into which they had been going to move when the bunkhouse had burned down and no sign of anyone near the corrals.

Someone was about, though. The front door of the bungalow was open, a dark, empty oblong that, now she was here, she was too scared to enter, and the windows were a lurid red in the light of the rapidly sinking sun. Together with the still remaining signs of the devastation caused by the fire, they gave the whole place an eerie, desolate look and the last shreds of her carefully nurtured optimism drained away.

She had been mad to come back. The journey to Calgary that had seemed so quick and effortless when she had flown there with Jay and Lori had taken almost the whole day. Hour upon hour of driving along the straight, virtually empty highway that ran from the Pacific to the Atlantic coasts, with only the occasional farm or truck stop and the specks of distant grazing animals to provide some distraction from the monotony.

The radio in the car hadn't worked, but her mind had and, as mile succeeded mile, what she was going back to do seemed even more impossible.

She was going back to tell Jay that she loved him when he considered her a liar and a cheat. In his eyes, she was a second Valerie, except that even his first wife had had the virtue of being honest. What had he said? That Valerie had never made any secret of the fact that, for her, her career came first, last and always.

Whereas she had deceived him. For her own amusement or to prove that she could do it, she had broken down the barriers with which he had protected his emotions ever since the failure of his marriage and she had then rejected him.

God knew it wasn't true, but that was how Jay saw it, and now those barriers had been rebuilt, could she ever tear them down again? Did she really need more proof than the completely expressionless rigidity of his face when he had got into the limousine at the Lancasters' to convince her that the door had shut, once and for ever, on his willingness to trust her with his love?

It had been hard not to turn off at one of the infrequent crossroads on the road back and drive as far and as fast as she could away from Rose Valley and the inevitable rejection that lay in store, and now that she was here, it was harder still to stay.

Dulcie got out and stood beside the car. It was so quiet that she could have been standing at the end of a dying world. She could see cattle in the distance, but nothing moved and nothing made a sound, and when she heard footsteps coming up behind her from the direction of the barns, she could scarcely summon the energy to turn round.

It wasn't Jay. If it had been, her breathing would already have been shallow and her whole being alive and aware. She didn't need eyes to know when Jay was close to her.

'You back?' The Lloyd Southwind who had met her at Winnipeg airport when she had first arrived had been positively welcoming compared to the Lloyd who was watching her when she finally turned around.

'Lloyd, where's Jay? I've got to talk to him!' She committed herself before she could back down.

'He's gone.' The foreman studied her with dark impassive eyes.

'Where?' A thousand answers came into her mind, but one stood out with sickening certainty. Jay had gone to New York. To Corinne!

'Down east. Mike's college is having an open day for students starting in the fall. Jay's flown him down and he's taken Lori with him.'

Dulcie put out a hand against the car; relief made her feel quite weak. 'When will they be back?'

'Dunno. Some time tomorrow, maybe.' Lloyd shrugged.

'Then I'll wait.' She reached inside the car for her bag.

'Jay didn't say nuthin' about that.' Lloyd's

clipped voice stopped her. 'And the men are all on round-up. You'd be here alone.'

'Lloyd,' she willed him to understand, 'I've got to wait! I've got to speak to Jay. He might have told you why.'

'He ain't told me nuthin'.' There was a long pause. 'He don't have to.' He turned away and walked off towards a jeep parked in the shadow of the barn and a few seconds later Dulcie was watching it disappear, leaving her quite alone.

There was food and there was shelter and there was a long night, and then, suddenly, there was the sound of a plane, in the distance at first but coming closer and touching down at the Rose Valley landing strip.

She wanted to run, blurt out an explanation before her courage failed her, but instead she forced herself to wait outside the house, shading her eyes against the midday sun as the plane landed and three figures got out. One turned in her direction and hesitated, and then Lori was rushing towards her and she was almost strangled by the force of thin arms wound around her neck.

'Dulcie! I knew you'd be back. Dad said I shouldn't expect you, but I *knew* all the time!' She turned a face filled with the satisfaction of proving herself right in the direction of her father. 'I told you, Dad, didn't I?'

'Yes, you did.' If Dulcie had hoped for any sign of welcome, she had been wrong. Jay's face was a mask; his eyes black stones. 'Dulcie probably doesn't like to leave anything unfinished.

What is there?' he asked her. 'Another two, or is it three, weeks before your three months here is up?'

'Jay, please!' Forgetting Lori, forgetting everything, she put out a hand and caught his arm as he started to go past, shocked by the contrast of the warmth of flesh and muscle and the absolute chill of eyes that flicked down on to her face.

'Lori,' Jay didn't take his eyes away, 'go and help Mike with the luggage. Now, what have you got to say?' he went on as Lori dragged reluctantly away. 'That you're sorry? That it was all a mistake? You don't have to tell me that—I already know.' His voice cracked. 'Isn't it enough that you've destroyed my peace of mind? What have you come back to do now—destroy me?' He moved away and her hand dropped to her side.

'Jay, please!' Her words trailed after him as he strode into the house.

It was amazing how you could go on carrying out a routine when your world was collapsing about your ears. Dulcie still got up each morning and went through the motions of helping Mike around the house. She even managed to sound enthusiastic when he told her about the college he would be starting within the next few weeks.

She still went riding with Lori after lessons in the afternoons and she still sat in her place at the long table in the dining room, eating food that was completely tasteless and facing a hostile stranger.

They even talked. Carrying on meaningless, trivial conversations for Lori's benefit when all the time what was left unsaid was hammering in Dulcie's mind.

As the days went past, her mood swung from anger to despair and she found herself both loving and hating Jay once more.

He was blaming her, and yet he had been the one to open up the floodgates to the emotions that had engulfed them both for a few, brief halcyon days. If he hadn't told her that he loved her, she could have kept her love a secret and gone back to England and to Ross.

No, not to Ross. That was something else that this faraway summer had changed. Ross now had his Kit. The only thing she had was her career.

One of the few positive tasks she did bring herself to achieve as the days dragged by was to write to Gerry and resign her post at the clinic.

At first she had thought of it as a lifeline, but she came to realise that its associations with Jay would make working there a constant, unbearable reminder of what might have been. It was there that she had first seen Jay, turning from the desk, annoyed at the interruption, when she had burst into Gerry's office unannounced. The moment she had opened that door had been the last before she had known that a man called Jason Maitland even existed, far less that he would come to dominate her life.

No, she could certainly not go back to the clinic and face those memories, but she still had the training and experience that made her a first-class child psychometrist. She could get another job and, who knew, one day she might actually wake up and find that she had not had Jay as her first conscious thought.

She took care with her letter to Gerry, explaining what had happened and about Ross. Gerry knew them all well enough to understand; it certainly would not be the first time that she had discussed her doubts about marrying Ross with him.

The plane was revving up when she finished her letter and she ran out, remembering the night she had run out after Jay and Corinne and firmly beating down the memory of what had happened next.

She waved and Lloyd opened the pilot's door as she ducked breathlessly underneath the wing.

'Lloyd, will you mail this for me?' She handed him the airmail letter.

'Sure!' All Jay's feelings were reflected in the impassive Indian face as Lloyd shut the door.

And then there were only days to wait. Days before the three months for which she was committed came to an end and she could leave Lori with an excuse and go back to England and pick up the threads of a life that would never be the same again.

Dulcie slammed her hair brush down on the dressing table. Was this really why she had come back from Calgary? Gerry would have got her letter by now. She no longer had a job. She had

nothing. Was she really going to let day after day
slip by until she could beat a civilised retreat?
Time spent, like that morning, hoping that the
pain would eventually become more bearable
while Jay went on building up the barrier of mistrust and groundless disbelief that separated them
until there was no hope of pulling it down.

She had a choice. Either she could let another
day go past or she could go and confront Jay
now, in the schoolroom, and force him to listen to
what she had to say.

Lori was not in the schoolroom. The voice she
had heard when she had briefly knocked and
walked in had been Jay on the schoolroom telephone extension. He was standing half turned
away from her and she couldn't see his face, but
she had the strangest feeling he might be talking
to Gerry.

Not that it mattered. What she had to concentrate on was how to maintain the courage that had
brought her this far. She could feel it draining
away, drop by drop, as she stood in the schoolroom doorway, aware of the tension in his shoulders as he held the telephone and guessing at the
brooding introspection on his face as he asked
sharp, direct questions, the sense of which was
drowned in the sound of blood pumping in her
ears.

Should she go or should she stay? The cow-
ardly part of her longed to give in to the conven-
tion that made it unseemly to eavesdrop on a private conversation. She could go away now and

come back later—or never, and the chance would be lost.

'It would seem, then, as if I've made something of a fool of myself again!' Jay's short, humourless laugh stopped her with the door half closed. '. . . . I hope you're right and that it's not too late . . . . No! Thanks for calling . . . fine, I'll let you know.'

He put the phone down and half turned towards Dulcie, stopping in mid-movement as he saw her for the first time and freezing her mind so that all the carefully prepared words and phrases vanished like raindrops after a desert storm.

What had she been going to say? That Ross had gone back to England to marry someone else? Even if he believed her, what difference would that make? He would probably think that she had come back to the ranch to make him her second choice.

She stood there, unable to speak or move, watching the play of expression on his face and scarcely noticing at first that it was changing from bleak despair to disbelief to joy.

And then she could no longer see his face. He had come towards her and swept her up in arms that held her as if they would never, ever let her go, and although she knew he would never hear the words she had waited so long to say, she said them just the same.

'Jay,' she whispered with her cheek against the wild beating of his heart, 'darling, I love you!'

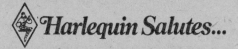